DEATH STALK . . .

The first two-leg, slightly crouched above her tracks, came abreast of The Hunter, then passed her. Then came two more two-legs, each grasping one of the horn-covered sticks that threw the deadly little black sticks; them, too, she allowed to pass.

The fourth was bigger than the others, which most likely meant he was the leader of the pack, thought The Hunter. Soundless as death, The Hunter hurled her weight upon this pack-leader. She growled deep satisfaction at the snapping of the neck. The warning had been given, first blood had been drawn, death had struck a blow at the Horseclans!

ROBERT ADAMS

THE CLAN OF THE CATS

A SIGNET BOOK

NEW AMERICAN LIBRARY

Copyright © 1988 by Robert Adams

SIGNET TRADEMARK REG. U.S. PAT. OFF. AND FOREIGN COUNTRIES
REGISTERED TRADEMARK—MARCA REGISTRADA
HECHO EN CHICAGO, U.S.A.

SIGNET, SIGNET CLASSIC, MENTOR, ONYX, PLUME, MERIDIAN
and NAL BOOKS are published by NAL PENGUIN INC.,
1633 Broadway, New York, New York 10019

First Printing, June, 1988

1 2 3 4 5 6 7 8 9

PRINTED IN THE UNITED STATES OF AMERICA

Chapter I

Icy-toothed wind soughed through the denuded branches of the overhanging trees, increasing the chill of an already-frigid day. Somewhere within the forest a branch exploded with the sharp crack of a pistol shot.

But the Hunter had never heard a shot of any kind and so ignored that sound as she did all natural sounds, concentrating the whole of her attention upon getting as close as possible to her browsing quarry before commencing the deadly rush and pounce that would, hopefully, result in her acquisition of almost her own weight of hot, bloody, delicious meat. Meat! Meat to fill the gnawing emptiness of her shrunken belly, meat enough, maybe, to be worried at by the three kittens waiting back in her den.

But the Hunter knew, too, that she must be close, very close, to have a chance, for she now had but three sound legs. Her left foreleg, deep-gored by the same shaggy-bull whose horns and stamping hooves had snuffed out the life of her mate, was healing but slowly in these days of deep snows and scant food.

As the manyhorn browser ambled a few feet farther and began to strip bark from yet another sapling, the Hunter carefully wriggled a few feet nearer, amber eyes fixed unwaveringly upon her prey, twitching nostrils seeking for the first faint odor of alarm or fear. Then, suddenly, the Hunter stopped, froze in place, even as the heads of all four browsers came up, swiveling to face a spot just a little to the Hunter's right.

The Hunter saw the muscles of the largest manyhorn bunch under the skin of his haunches. But before he could essay even the first wild leap away from the danger all sensed, a volley of little thin black sticks came hissing from the thick cover of a stand of mountain laurel and all four of the browsers collapsed, kicking their razor-edged hooves at empty air, one of them coughing quantities of frothy blood forth to sink, steaming, into the deep, white snow.

A vagrant puff of wind wafted to the Hunter the rare but still-hated scent of two-legs, and her lip curled in a soundless snarl. *They* were trying to rob her of *her* manyhorns, trying to rob her and her helpless cubs of life itself, for if she did not have food, she knew that she soon would lack the strength to get food, and her kittens were still too young to hunt for themselves. Outside the den and without her protection, they would be the hunted rather than the hunters.

The lung-shot browser, a hornless doe, struggled to her feet and staggered across the tiny glade. Another of the hissing black sticks sped out of the laurel covert, *thunnk* into her heaving flank, and she fell again, this time almost under the Hunter's paws. The heady scent of her hot blood filled the Hunter's nostrils and set her stomach to growling, while her tongue unconsciously sought her furry lips.

* * *

Dik Esmith unstrung his short, powerful recurved bow and replaced it in his bowcase quiver. The other three archers emulated their leader, while Dik mindcalled back to where the rest of the hunting party waited with the horses.

"Uncle Milo, brothers, once more has Clan Esmith demonstrated for all to see the matchless skill at stealth and the deadly accuracy of its bowmen—"

"And," broke in a mindspeak that Dik recognized as that of Rahn Linsee, "the longwinded boasting for which Clan Esmith is justly famous. Get to the point, Dik—did you and your blunderers kill the deer or not?"

Dik's horny hand unconsciously sought the well-worn hilt of the saber he had left behind at the beginning of his stalk. "*Blunderers*, is it? I had always thought, Linsee, that that title was exclusive to Clan Linsee . . . along with 'cowards.' "

"Enough, *children,* enough!" Command was unmistakable in a third and exceptionally powerful mindspeak. "We are out this wretched day to kill game to feed our folk, not to carelessly begin bloodfeuds. How many deer, Dik?"

"Four, Uncle Milo. But the Linsee filth started it. He had no right to—"

"*Enough*, I said!" came Milo's retort. "Perhaps I should have been certain I brought men to hunt with me. You do all look like men, you bear the weapons of men, but just now you put me in mind of pugnacious herd boys wrangling over a sickly heifer. Next time I might be better off to bring a few maiden archers, eh?"

"I . . . I'm sorry, Uncle Milo," beamed Dik sheepishly. "But he—"

"No 'buts'!" Milo's thought beam cracked like a whip. "Rahn was simply joking, *weren't you, Rahn Linsee?*"

"I . . . oh, yes, yes, of course, Uncle Milo, I was joshing dear Brother Dik."

"And you are lying in your teeth," thought Milo to himself. "You were deliberately trying to provoke a fight with the Esmiths because I chose to bring their archers rather than Linsee bowmen on this hunt. But," he smiled to himself, "those are my Horseclansmen for you; if there're no outsiders around to fight, they'll hop at each other's throats.

"Be that as it may, though," he thought on, "I must have done more than a few somethings right, over the years, else you and your cousin would not be around to snarl and snap at each other. A bare hundred years ago, thousands, millions of people lived hereabouts, and now you could ride for weeks in any direction and not meet any human who does not claim kinship to one of the Horseclans. And I doubt that all fifty-odd clans together number as many as five thousand souls.

"I think we're somewhere in northern Nevada, or maybe it's southern Idaho. A century back, great, glittering, thoroughly modern cities reared out of the desert to the south of us—hell, they even raised crops in places where we'd now lose all our herds from thirst and hunger were we crazy enough to try to make it across.

"Who could ever have imagined, back then, that ten dozen scared, ragged, starving kids could not only survive the death of the world into which they'd been born, but that their direct descendants could so well adapt to a hideously hostile environment and become fearless, self-reliant men like these?"

*   *   *

The Hunter flattened her long-furred body to the snowy ground and moved not a whisker, for she wanted none of the black sticks coming at her. But neither was she willing to leave so much meat, either.

She watched four two-legs, covered in animal hides and furs, rise up from the shrubs that had hidden them. Pulling out long, shiny things, they went from one to another of the downed manyhorns, cutting open the big throat veins and holding hollow horns to catch the hot red blood, which they then drank off with smiles and relish.

The Hunter could hear other two-legs and the rather stupid, hornless four-legs that often carried them on their backs coming closer from upwind. If she was to have any chance of getting clear with one of those dead manyhorns, it must be done quickly.

The first four two-legs had stopped drinking blood, and now three of them were dragging the largest manyhorn toward a large tree on the other side of the glade. The fourth was shinnying up the bole, a rawhide rope clenched between his teeth.

The Hunter had wormed herself to the very limit of available concealment. Only a partially snow-covered log and a body-length of open ground now lay between her and the dead doe. With careful speed, she drew her powerful hinder legs beneath her, then sprang over the log, landing almost beside the carcass.

Rahn Linsee strode into the glade, just behind Uncle Milo. Though big for his breed, Rahn still was a head shorter than Milo Moray. The other differences between the one man and the others were not so easily apparent, not that any Horseclansman or woman would have even considered questioning said differences. They all had known or known of Uncle Milo all their lives—he did not winter with the same clans every year. Their parents had known him all their lives, and their grandparents and all their ancestors back to the very Sacred Ancestors whom Uncle Milo had succored and led upon the path to their present greatness.

Uncle Milo never changed. Horseclansmen might be born, toddle about the camps between the felt yurts, guard the herds until their war training was complete, then ride the raid and take heads or booty or women; they might then die, full of glory and glorious memories, surrounded at the last by their get and the get of their get. But Uncle Milo would be the same tall, black-haired and dark-eyed man who had drunk the health at their birth.

Mothers told curious children that Uncle Milo was a god. That he was the only god to survive the awesome War of the Gods. As the children grew older, they found it hard to consciously believe godhood of this man who rode and ate and drank with them, slept in their yurts, often swived an offered young wife or concubine, who sweated and bled and defecated like any other man. But in their subconscious, the teachings of childhood were often strong.

But no less strong was Rahn Linsee's pugnacity. "Hi, Dik Esmith! Always has it been said that the Esmith clan were a mite slow of thought, but only a very stupid man cannot tell the difference between three dead deer and four dead deer. Or did you have all ten fingers tucked up your arse to keep them warm, eh?"

Uncaring that his tormentor went fully armed with saber and dirk at his belt, Dik spun about from the hung buck he had been flaying, took two running steps and flung himself upon Rahn, seeking to get his teeth, nails or blood-slimed skinning knife into the hated flesh.

At Milo's impatient mindspeak and gesture, the rest of the party lifted the battling men, jerked them apart most ungently and prudently disarmed them both.

Milo strode before them, scowling darkly. "Damn you both! Your chiefs shall hear of this, from *me!* While you are in camp, I don't care if you blind, maim or chop each other into gobbets, but a raid or a hunt is no place for personal grudge-fighting, and you both are old enough and experienced enough to know that fact. What in hell kind of example do you think you're setting for these younger warriors, eh? Do you even care?

"Your ancestors knew better, knew that their folk were only so strong as their ties—blood and kin—one to the other. Are their descendants then idiots? The hand of every Dirtman, every non-Kindred wanderer, is against the Horseclans. As if those were not enemies enough, the very elements would deny you and your herds life."

He motioned that the men be released. "Dik Esmith, Rahn Linsee, this winter has been very hard and is lasting much longer than most. We dare not take much milk, now, because the calves need it, but our folk must have food. These deer could mean the difference between life and death for some. So let's get about preparing them for packing before the wolves scent all this fresh blood."

As the men began to move off, he raised his voice in a parting admonition. "And hear me, I'll put my saber through the next selfish roughneck who tries to start a fight here."

When the three deer were all hung and cleaned and the meat and other usable portions wrapped in their own hides and lashed on to the packhorses, Milo, Dik and Rahn examined the bloody spot on which the missing doe had lain. Several large pugmarks were deeply pressed into the snow.

"Puma?" mused Rahn, aloud.

Dik snorted. "No puma ever grew feet *that* big, nor any lynx, either." He scratched after a flea under his parka hood. "But . . . maybe one of those spotted cats the southern Dirtmen call teegrai?"

Milo shook his head. "No, this animal is a little bigger and a good deal heavier—if those tracks are any indication—than any jaguar or *tigre* I ever saw." Reaching over to a fallen log, he pulled several long, silky hairs from where they had caught in the rough bark. They were a creamy buff for most of their length, tipped with a dark grey.

He stood, and the two Horseclansmen emulated him. "Rahn, take all but three of your men and go back to camp with that meat. I'm going after that cat—whatever kind it is, I think its pelt would make a handsome saddlecover. Besides, it did steal our deer. I'll take Dik, two of his bowmasters, and a couple of your spearmen with me. The other two men can stay here in the clearing and guard the horses until we get back."

A hundred yards into the thickening forest, the Hunter could no longer resist the temptation. Dropping her burden at the base of a tall pine, she used her daggerlike fangs to rip open the doe's belly, then tore out greedy mouthfuls of the tender, still-hot viscera.

From behind a bush, a vixen thrust out her wriggling black button of a nose and a couple of inches of her silvery-grey jaws. The Hunter placed her good forepaw atop the dark brown carcass and rippled a snarl of warning. The nose and jaws disappeared and the vixen scurried away . . . but not far; she knew her turn would come and she had the patience to await it.

The sharpest pangs of hunger temporarily assuaged, the Hunter arose, gripped her somewhat lighter burden, and limped on toward the isolated stand of rocks wherein lay her den and her hungry kittens.

When the Hunter was well out of sight among the dark boles of the trees, the vixen crept from beneath the snow-laden bush and first cleaned up every scrap of gut or organ, then began to lap at the bloody snow.

With Rahn Linsee and the bulk of the hunters on their way back to the two-clan camp, Milo and the remaining men unsaddled their horses, then broke down squaw-wood to build a fire for those who would remain in the glade with the animals. That done, they set out on the clear track of the big cat with its stolen deer.

They had only gone a few yards when Djim Linsee, a gifted tracker, squatted over the pugmarks and said, "Uncle Milo, this cat may be big, but it's hurt, too."

Milo squatted beside the broken-nosed towhead. "How can you be sure, Djim?"

The tracker pointed a grubby forefinger at first one, then another print. "You see how deep and clear this track is, Uncle Milo? And how shallow and fuzzy is this one? The cat's putting as little weight as possible on the left leg. It must be a really big cat, though, and very strong, to drag so big a deer so easily with only three legs."

They went on cautiously, the bowmen with their weapons strung, one arrow nocked and one or two others between the fingers of the bowhand. The spearmen followed close behind, hefting the balance of their six-foot wolf spears. Milo had armed himself with three stout, yard-long darts. Like the others, he had hung his saber diagonally across his back to keep it out of the way in the thick forest.

The vixen's keen ears heard their approach long before they came into view, and she was nowhere about when they arrived at the base of the big pine.

Djim squatted, picked up a shred of gut missed by the grey vixen, rubbed it between his fingers, sniffed at it and then tasted it. His pale-blue eyes on the ground, he said, "The cat stopped here, Uncle Milo, tore the deer open and ate most of the innards. Then . . ."

He fell silent, then bent over to peer closely at a patch of snow that looked to Milo like any other. Extending his tongue, the towhead tasted some near-invisible something, then straightened, grinning. "Uncle Milo, the cat is a she-cat and likely is nursing kittens. That stain there where she laid is milk, cat milk."

"After she ate her fill of the deer's innards, she headed that way." He swept his arm to the northwest. "Then a grey fox was here to pick up her leavings."

As they trudged on after the cat, Milo thought: "Damn! That man is no more than twenty-five years old, yet he's acquired knowledge and skills, a keenness of smell and an acuity of vision that I've not picked up in the hundred fifty-plus years I've been around." Then he mentally shrugged. "Maybe I never will become as these people of my fashioning. I think it's the early life, the formative years. Mine were spent—to the best of my knowledge, of course; damn, there's always that memory lapse or whatever to screw up my calculations!—in a degree of urban civilization that these fine men could not even imagine and which, were they suddenly put down in it, they would find terrifying and abhorrent."

He thought hard, thought back and back, trying to dredge from out his memory the America of the last quarter of the twentieth century. He sought to recall how it was nearly eightscore years now past, before most of the nation's two hundred millions were returned to the dust, before the cities and towns were become only ruins, crumbling and overgrown.

At last, he desisted. He could evoke a dim ghost of a memory, but no more. It had just been too long; too many more recent scenes overlay that long-dead past now. Funny, he could easily remember women he had had, back then, in some detail, could recall the performance of fine cars and boats he had owned, but still the broader picture of that lost world eluded him.

"Just as well, likely," he muttered under his breath. "Let the dead stay buried. They'd be as lost in this time and environment as we would be in theirs."

The bowman ahead of him in the single file half turned. "Yes, Uncle Milo . . . ?" he mindspoke.

Milo smiled, and answered as silently, "Never mind, Pat. I was talking to myself."

The ground was harder underfoot, under the layers of snow; the men's bootsoles now frequently slipped on the surfaces of rocks and boulders thrusting up from out of the frozen earth, forcing them to throw out their arms for balance or grasp at trees and shrubs for support.

At an overly thick copse of brush and trees, the spoor veered to the right, and the hunters relentlessly followed it.

The Hunter was aware of her pursuit very soon after it commenced, since her pursuers made almost as much noise as a stampeding herd of shaggy bulls. But she was easily maintaining her lead, despite the weakness and lancing agony that her left foreleg was become with the strain of dragging the stiffening, heavy carcass through the breast-deep snow and over the rough ground beneath it. Only when she neared the hillock atop which lay her den did she decide to take action against the persistent two-legs. Perhaps if she killed one of the pack, the others would feed on him as wolves did, and give her time to cover her trail to the den.

The Hunter had never had much contact with two-legs, but she had seen her mother killed by them, pierced through and through with the hateful little black sticks, then pinned to the ground, still snarling and snapping and clawing, by a longer stick in the hands of a two-leg sitting high on the back of a hornless four-leg. She did hate two-legs, did the Hunter, but she also respected them, so she laid her ambush with care.

She continued well past the spot she had chosen, then adroitly broke her trail by leaping atop a fallen tree bole from which the night winds had scoured the snow. Climbing atop the mass of dead roots and frozen earth, the Hunter reared to her full length and carefully hung her precious deer over the broad branch of a still-standing tree. Below that branch, the trunk stood bare and the bark was slippery, so the carcass should be safe from the depredations of any other predator save perhaps a bear or another cat. And the only bear that stalked hereabouts was denned up a full day's run to the north. The few small cats ran in mortal fear of the Hunter and would never venture so close to her den.

The soil was thin and rocky on the hillslope, and over the years many a tree had fallen to storms and winds. The Hunter now made use of these raised ways to make her way back to the ambush point she had chosen without leaving telltale tracks in the snow. Arriving at last in the thick brush, she bellied down and made a swift and silent passage to the opposite side of the copse. There she crouched, motionless as the tree trunks themselves, waiting.

The first two-leg, slightly crouched above her tracks, came abreast of the Hunter, then passed her, a long shiny-tipped stick dangling from one forepaw. Then came two two-legs, each grasping one of the horn-covered sticks that threw the deadly little black sticks; them, too, she allowed to pass around the point of the copse.

The third was bigger than the others, which most likely meant that he was leader of the pack, thought the Hunter. He bore neither long stick nor short, but three of an intermediate length. Soundless as death itself, the Hunter hurled her weight upon this pack leader. Even as she bore him to earth, she thrust her good, right forepaw around his head, hooked her big claws into the flesh over the jaw, then jerked sharply back and to the right.

The Hunter growled deep satisfaction at the snapping of the neck. Then she spun upon her haunches and bounded back into the brush-grown copse, leaving the other two-legs shouting behind her. Many of the little black sticks were hurled after her, but only one of the hastily aimed missiles fleshed, and that one only split the tip of her ear before hissing on to rattle among the tree trunks.

Well satisfied with her strategem, the Hunter negotiated the width of the copse and made her way back to where she had cached her deer, directly this time, for there now was no need to hide her spoor. Soon she and her three kittens would be feasting upon tasty deer flesh, while the two-legs would probably be tearing at the carcass of their dead leader.

*   *   *

Milo could not repress a groan as Dik Esmith dabbed a bit of homespun cloth at the hot blood gushing from the claw-torn cheek.

"Let be, Dik, let be," he gasped. "That cat is not only canny, she's strong as a horse. She broke my neck like a dry twig, but it will knit quickly enough. Just leave me here.

"She's most likely broken trail, so some of you had better scout around and see where the spoor takes up again. Djim, you and a couple of bowmen backtrack her through that copse, but be damned careful—you've all seen what she can do."

Milo lay still, feeling the pains of regeneration of bone and tissue already commencing. He was aware that Dik and one other squatted nearby, unwilling to leave him hurt and alone in this cold and dangerous place.

"They're good men," he thought, "all of them. I'm glad it was me that that wily flea factory chose as victim, and not one of them. In thirty minutes, those tears in my cheek will be fading scars and even the vertebrae will be sound again in an hour or less. But if she'd jumped one of them, we'd be bearing a well-dead Linsee or Esmith back to camp."

For the many-thousandth time he wondered what had made him the kind of being he was, wondered if he was unique on the earth, or if, somewhere, there might be others of his kind. Over the course of the hundred fifty-odd years of life he could remember, he had suffered wounds enough to have slain a hundred ordinary men—he had been gunshot, stabbed, slashed, cut and clubbed. Once an axe had taken off his left hand above the wrist, but it had regrown; twice he had lost the same ear, yet he now had two.

With an agonizing tingle, life was coming back into his arms and legs and body. When he could easily flex his limbs and abdominal muscles, Milo rose to sit propped on his hands.

Shortly Djim Linsee approached and proffered a horn cup of clear, icy water. Milo gulped the fluid gratefully.

The tracker sank down before him. "There are many fallen trees just beyond this place, Uncle Milo. The cat must have doubled back across them, for we could only find the tracks she made when she ran away. She had hung the deer up in a tree, and after she took it down, she went uphill at an angle to the right until she came to flowing water. The stream bed is all rock, so where she went from there, upstream or down, is anybody's guess. But I have a feeling . . ."

"That she went upstream?" asked Milo.

Djim nodded quickly. "Cats always seek high places. I climbed a tree on the stream bank and looked uphill. The slope is very much steeper farther on, but the top of the hill is flat and level and virtually treeless. Near the center of the hilltop is a high and spreading pile of rocks. True, I could not see any openings that looked big enough for such a cat to go into, but then I could only see the one side.

"Don't ask me how, Uncle Milo, but I *know* her den is in there, in those rocks!"

Chapter II

But when Milo stood up, he nearly fell again. Seeing him so unsteady, Dik and Djim half-led, half-carried him up to the bank of the little stream. With his charge seated against the thick bole of an elderly oak, Dik mindspoke his clansmen to gather squaw-wood, brought steel and stone and tinder from out his beltpouch and soon had the dry stuff smoking quickly.

For some time, they had been hearing, now and again, the howling of wolves, but such was not an unusual sound either upon high plains or mountains. In the dead of a hard winter such as this, the packs often joined into superpacks and hunted almost constantly, day and night, small game or big, resting only on those rare occasions that their bellies had a modest quantity of food to work upon.

However, the howls of this pack were becoming louder, and that meant *nearer*! Now and again, gusts of wind bore the excited yelping of wolves on a fresh trail . . . and no man in the party had the slightest doubt about just whose trail those gaunt grey demons were on.

Once, long ago, Milo had faced a big wolfpack, while afoot, in open country. He had come out of it alive and whole, but more than half the score or so of warriors he had started with had not been so lucky, and even those who lived had carried scars of that fearsome battle to their graves.

Milo forced himself erect and set himself to control the shakiness of his legs. "Dik, Djim, the rest of you, this is no fit place to try to fight off Wind knows how many wolves. And we number too few, even were the conditions ideal.

"Now, true, we could each climb a tree and rope ourselves into it, but we could very easily freeze to death, so exposed this coming night, or die of hunger or thirst before those stubborn devils left.

"Djim, you say that the hill ahead is steep. How steep?"

The intuitive tracker sensed his embryonic plan and shook his shaggy blond head. "Not that steep, Uncle Milo. We won't be able to go up as easily as a cat, and the wolves will have even more trouble, but they and we will be able to climb it."

"Then how about the rocks on the summit, Djim?"

The tracker closed his eyes and wrinkled his brow in concentration, then opened them with an incisive nod of his head. "Yes, Uncle Milo, the rocks are all overgrown with vines, but there are places that are almost sheer for seven or eight feet or more near the very top. And the top looks to have a depression in the center, so it may offer some protection from the winds."

The way was steep, very steep, and might have been deadly treacherous in better, warmer weather, but now, at least, the jumbled blackish rocks were frozen into place and only a few shifted under the weights of the climbing men. The sounds from behind spurred their straining muscles to further efforts. The wolves had reached the stream now, and were fanning out to find the place where the men had come out of the swift-flowing water.

Milo alone recognized the rocks up which they frantically scrambled for what they were—much-weathered shards of old asphalt. A hundred years ago this had no doubt been part of a road leading to the hilltop, but fivescore freezing winters and as many scorching summers had buckled and cracked it. Then, undercut by erosion, the easy, manmade gradient had given way, the fill had washed down to the base of the hillock and left behind the heavier chunks of paving.

Milo led the way, knowing that any rock that would bear his weight would certainly not give under the lighter men who followed him. As he pulled himself over the rim, he heard the triumphant signaling howl of a wolf, a wolf that had sniffed out their trail. Now bare seconds were precious as rubies.

Djim Linsee was the next to clamber onto the level ground, and he and Milo grasped the arms of each of the others as they came into reach and pulled them up by main strength, bidding them run for the stone ruin—for such Milo could see it to be—some eighty yards across the tiny mesa. But even as they raised the last man, Dik Esmith, the first of the wolves ran snarling to the foot of the incline, there to rear on his hind legs and voice his savage view-halloo.

Djim snatched up a piece of loose stone as big as his two fists and hurled it with all his wiry strength and with deadly accuracy. His narrow skull shattered, the big dog-wolf fell without even a whimper, to lie twitching below them. But his last howl had been heard and understood. An increasing chorus of wolf-sounds told Milo and Djim of the grey death coming on as fast as the hunger-driven beasts could run.

In her den, full of deer meat and languidly laving her kittens with her wide red tongue, having to hold the squirming bundles of soft fur down with her good forepaw, the Hunter had heard the wolves afar off, long before the less sensitive ears of the two-legs could have been aware of the huge pack.

But the Hunter knew herself to be safe, even should the pack ascend the hill. Even with an injured forepaw, the big cat realized that she was more than a match for any one wolf, and no more then one wolf at a time could crawl into the narrow, winding passage that led to this den. Too, her eyes were better adapted to the near-total darkness that prevailed beyond the first couple of turns of the passage.

Three winters ago, she and her now-dead mate had lazily taken turns at killing wolves starved or crazed enough to enter the confines of that passage. As many had they killed as she had claws on her forepaws, and as fast as the cats' mighty buffets crushed skulls or snapped necks, as fast as their long fangs tore out throats, so fast did others of the pack drag out their dead or dying fellows to tear them apart in an orgy of lupine cannibalism.

At last, though, the edges of their hunger slightly dulled by their grisly repast, the pack had trotted off to seek out less dangerous prey. And the Hunter, gently swishing her long, thick tail and watching the kittens' wobbling stalks and bumbling leaps at the tailtip with a critical maternal eye, knew that she was still capable of defending herself and her young from any number of wolves.

*   *   *

The building that was now become but ruin had been fashioned of bricks and rough-hewn blocks of granite. Milo could see no clues as to what had caused the collapse of the structure, but he was not really looking. Djim and another extraordinarily agile man had somehow gotten atop the almost smooth, almost vertical eight-foot-plus wall, and Milo was now using his prodigious strength to lift the other four, one by one, holding them at arm's length over his head, that those above might drag them up.

The wolfpack was howling and yelping below the hill. A few had already scrabbled up the difficult ascent and were even now racing flat out toward the ruin, howling back the message that the quarry were in sight. The last Horseclansman raised and safe on high, Milo stepped back a couple of paces and leaped upward, his arms stretched upward toward the hands that reached for him. But his legs failed to deliver their usual power and even collapsed under him as he fell back, sending him tumbling down to the very foot of the ruin.

Only fifty feet distant was the nearest wolf—its red tongue lolling over its cruel white fangs, short spurts of mist jetting from its nostrils, and pure murder shining from yellow eyes.

Milo fought back onto his feet and retraced his way to the foot of the sheer wall. Even as he reached it and grasped the joined belts the Horseclansmen had lowered, he could hear the claws of the big wolf clicking on exposed surfaces of the ruin. The animal's panting sounded unbelievably loud and Milo even imagined that he could feel the hot, dank breath on the back of his neck.

As the Horseclansmen drew him up, he freed his right hand and drew his saber, for he sensed himself rising very slowly, too slowly. His head and shoulders already were above the upper edge of the ruin when the wolf arrived where he had been. Without any discernible pause, the ravenous beast jumped high, jaws agape.

The wolf's first jump missed, but then so did the swing of Milo's saber. On the second jump, the slavering jaws brushed Milo's bootsole, but his keen-edged saber took off most of one furry ear, and with the surprised yelp of a kicked dog, the wolf fell back. The determined animal essayed one more leap, but by then Milo's legs were disappearing over the top edge of the ruin.

They were safe for the moment, but as more and more grey shapes debouched onto the mesa it became more and ever more clear that their situation was distinctly unenviable.

The wall up which they had come was the lowest side of the tower, so they were at least safe from wolves, so long as they stayed on high. However, although the tower top was slightly concave, the floor was only bare inches below the jagged rim, offering no trace of protection from wind, which, judging from the rime of ice and lack of snow, must be vicious and biting here, so high.

Nor was there anything burnable. While each man carried a few ounces of fatty pemmican in his belt pouch, none had more than enough for one full day. Moreover, none of them had brought water bottles, knowing that they could slake their thirst with snow, but this eyrie was bare of snow.

Husbanding their bare dozen arrows against greater need, the Horseclansmen used their heavy-bladed dirks to work loose jagged chunks of granite and weather-worn bricks, then they and Milo spent the rest of the waning daylight teaching the wolves to keep a respectable distance from the tower.

Horseclansmen were ever prone to gambling, they would

wager on anything, and Uncle Milo was asked to bear witness to numerous bets while the supply of missiles lasted—cattle, weapons, old bits of gaudy loot, even women and horses. At least a dozen wolves were either killed outright or so badly crippled that they could not flee or fight off the packmates that savaged them and devoured their sometimes living flesh.

The night was terrible. Rolling pebbles in their mouths to allay their thirst, the nomads laced their hoods tightly and drew the woolen blizzard masks up over lips and vulnerable noses. In the very center of the concavity, they huddled together for warmth, frequently changing position that all might have equal time in the warmer, centermost position.

Not that sleep was easy, for the wolves paced and howled, snuffled and barked and yelped throughout the long, dark night. Wolf after wolf set himself at the sheer walls, jumping and falling back to jump again until exhaustion claimed him. The pack seemed driven mad by the smell of so much manflesh and blood, so near, yet so unattainable to them.

Light came at last, but there was no visible sun and no cessation of the biting wind. The signs were unmistakable that a blizzard was building up. Milo knew that were he and his men to survive the coming weather, they *must* get off this exposed pinnacle and into shelter of some kind. But how?

The wolves paced the length and breadth of the little mesa. They numbered at least threescore, possibly more—grey wolves and those of a dirty brown color, with here and there a black one. Milo could almost feel pity for the canines, for they were obviously starving, with ribracks clearly visible beneath the dull, matted coats.

The pack had lost their fear of hurled stones in the night and once more were ranging close about the tower. But the men discovered that there were few loose rocks remaining on the rims; only in the center, where their combined body heat had thawed the rubble to a degree, could they pry up broken bricks and shards of grey granite.

With the supply of rocks decreasing, Milo awarded such as were available to the four most accurate hunters—Dik, Djim, and the tracker's two younger brothers, fiery-haired twins called Bili and Bahb. Milo and the other Horseclansmen set themselves and their dirks to worrying loose more of the bits and pieces of old masonry littering the center of the tower.

Milo thrust his dirk blade under a brick that looked to be almost whole . . . and *felt his blade ring on metal!* He set the other men to working upon the same area, and slowly a pitted, red-brown iron ring was exposed. Shortly, they had cleared the two-foot-square trapdoor in which the ring was set.

One of the Horseclansmen took a grip upon the ring and heaved, then grasped it afresh with both hands, gritted his teeth and strained until the throbbing veins bulged in his forehead, but the rust-streaked door never budged.

"Wait," counseled Milo. "There may be a catch of some kind holding it shut." His dirk blade proved too wide for the crack at the edge closest to the ring; so too was the blade of his skinning knife. But the blade of the small dagger he habitually carried in his boot top slipped easily in. Even with the center of the ring, the blade encountered an obstruction; while pushing the knife against the unseen object, Milo noted that the ring turned a millimeter or so. Maintaining knife pressure, he gripped the ring in his other hand and twisted it right, then left, then right again. At the last twist, the obstruction was gone, and the blade slid easily from corner to corner of the door.

"Try it now."

The Horseclansman heaved. There was momentary resistance, then, with an unearthly squeal and a shower of rust, the door rose jerkily upward to disclose the first treads of what looked to Milo like a steel stairway, covered with dust and cobwebs.

When the nomad's belts were once more formed into a makeshift belt and knotted to the back of his own belt, Milo gingerly set foot to the ancient stairs, saber slung on his back and big dirk ready in his hand. As the Horseclansmen watched, all huddled about the opening into the unknown, Milo disappeared into the darkness, only the ring of his bootsoles on the metal telling them that he was still descending.

A sudden intensification of the hot lancing pain in her left foreleg awakened the Hunter, that and a thirst that was raging. Arising, she hobbled across the high-ceilinged, airy den to lap avidly at the pool in one corner—a pool that never froze even in the worst of winters and that never had been dry even in the most arid of summers.

Her thirst quenched in the crackling-cold water, the Hunter hobbled back to her guard post by the mouth of the tunnel. Lying down once more, for she seemed utterly devoid of energy, she licked at her swollen, throbbing left foreleg. Even the gentle touch of her tongue sent bolts of burning agony through every fiber of her being . . . and, of course, that was when she heard the first wolf enter the tunnel.

The Hunter had been aware that the two-legs were upon the high, flat place, where birds nested in warmer times, and where she and her now-dead mate had right often sunned themselves. But because she did know the place so well, she knew that there was no danger of the two-legs getting from there to the den. And if the wolves could find a way to get to the two-legs and wanted to eat them, they were more than welcome. As for her, she had nearly gagged at the foul stench of that two-leg she had so easily killed on the preceding day.

When the clawclicks and shufflings told her that the lupine invader was past the first turn of the passage, she entered it herself, putting as little weight as possible upon her strangely huge and very tender left foreleg.

They met between the first turn and the second, in a section too low-ceilinged for either to stand fully erect. The Hunter knew that she possessed the deadly advantage here, for with only toothy jaws for weapons, the wolf could only lunge for her throat, whereas a single blow of her claw studded forepaw could smash the life from him as quickly as she had killed that two-leg. But she reckoned without her disability.

Sensing more than seeing the location of the wolf's head, she lashed out with her sound paw . . . but this suddenly transferred the full weight of her head and forequarters onto the hot, swollen left foreleg. Squalling with pain, she stumbled, and her buffet failed to strike home; the bared claws only raked the wolf's head and mask, and before she could recover, his crushing jaws had closed upon her one good foreleg, eyeteeth stabbing, carnassials scissoring flesh and cracking bone.

But before the wolf could raise his bloody head, the Hunter had closed, had sunk her own huge fangs into the sinewy neck and crushed the lupine spine.

As the wolf's jaws relaxed in death, the Hunter slowly

backed down the tunnel, dragging her two useless fore-paws, growling deep in her throat as the waves of pain washed over her. Weak and growing weaker, she tumbled the two-foot drop from tunnel mouth to den floor.

Two of the kittens, trailed by the third, bounced merrily over to her, but a growled command sent them scurrying back into a far, dark corner. The Hunter knew that she and they were doomed now. She might have enough strength remaining to kill with her fangs the next wolf that came out of the tunnel. But there would be another behind him, and another and another, and the one she proved too weak to kill would kill her. Then the pack would be at the helpless kittens, ripping the little bodies to shreds, eating them alive.

Deciding to guard her young as long as possible, the Hunter painfully dragged herself across the den and took her death-stand before them.

The steel staircase was spiral, and though it trembled and creaked and crackled under his weight, Milo made it safely to the bottom. Untying the belts from his own, he mindspoke the men above him.

"The stairs will hold you, but don't come down yet. This room seems small. See if that door will open wider, then get back from it. It's dark as pitch down here."

The hinges screamed like a damned soul, but finally the Horseclansmen got the trapdoor almost flat on the roof. In the increased light, Milo could see that the chamber was, indeed, small, a bit smaller than the roof above. Every surface was covered with a century of dust and hung with a hundred years' worth of cobwebs. But he could spot no droppings of any kind, so apparently no animal or bird had ever gained access to it.

It took him a moment to remember just what the dust-shrouded object sitting on a shelf at waist level was: it was a gasoline lantern.

"I wonder . . ." Brushing away the dust and cobwebs, he could see that the artifact was not rusted, being finished in chrome or stainless steel; the glass was intact and there was even a filament still in place. Lifting the object, he shook it beside his ear. It sloshed almost full, and if that liquid was gasoline . . .

Finding the handle of the air pump, he tried it. The shaft moved smoothly in the tube. Now if he'd just had a match.

He let his fingers wander the length of the shelf. Near the edge they encountered a small metal cylinder. Not daring to hope, Milo brought his new find into the light. It was badly rusted, and it was all that he could do to coax the screwtop loose.

"Sonofabitch." He breathed softly. The cylinder was filled with matches, the heads each coated with wax.

With the trapdoor closed and seven bodies gathered in close quarters, the nomads soon ceased to shiver and exclaimed upon the clear, intensely bright light of the lantern. A lighted exploration discovered another, larger lantern, two corroded and useless flashlights, a two-gallon can of lantern fuel, an assortment of rusty machine tools, and a holstered revolver, now just a single lump of rusty metal.

There was one other find. Set in the concrete floor near the foot of the stairs was another trapdoor, about three feet by two. Milo filled and lit the larger lantern, took the smaller for himself, then opened the second trapdoor to disclose more steel stairs, but these looking to be in better condition.

"Dik, Djim, you and the men stay here. I'll mindcall if

I need you or when I find food or water. Leave that thing in the leather holder alone. It was once a dangerous weapon and still might hurt or kill one of you if you tinker with it.''

The floor at the bottom of the second spiral stairs was also concrete, but it had once been covered with asphalt tile, which cracked and powdered under Milo's boots. To his left, grown over with plant roots, was a jumble of brick and stone, and Milo guessed that he was probably within the main ruin, whereon the tower sat perched.

Behind and to his right were plain, sound brick walls, still partially covered with remnants of rotted wood paneling. More of the rotted wood framed the door ahead of him, its brass knob pale-green with verdigris. The knob turned stiffly in his hand, but the door remained closed. Setting the light on the stairs, he put both hands to the task. Something popped and the door swung open.

The door led into a small, narrow room, the left side of it lined with closed metal cabinets, the right taken up by a flight of concrete stairs leading down. All of the cabinets proved bare of much that was still usable—a few brass buckles, a handful of metal buttons; perhaps the nails and eyelets could be salvaged from the several pairs of rotting boots by the metal-thrifty clansmen.

As he opened the last cabinet, he jumped back and cursed at unexpected movement, his hand going to the hilt of his dirk. The big brown rat struck the floor running and scuttled down the steps, only to come back up twice as fast, shrieking in terror and streaking directly between Milo's feet to leap into a hole in the wall.

Thus warned, Milo descended the stairs slowly and carefully, holding the lantern high. It was well that he had done so. The bare concrete of the small room below was littered with nearly two dozen sluggishly writhing rattle-snakes!

"Well," thought Milo, "that answers the food problem." But none of the vipers lay between the foot of the stairs and the closed door in the facing wall, so he left them alone.

This door was the hardest to open he had encountered, but at last he did so, to find himself faced with a short stretch of corridor and three more doors, one in each wall. He entered and closed the door behind him.

The doors to both left and right were secured with heavy padlocks. Stenciled on the face of the left door was "FALL-OUT SHELTER—KEEP OUT—THIS MEANS YOU!" On the face of the right was "PRIVATE SANCTUM OF STATION DIRECTOR—TRESPASSERS WILL BE BRUTALLY VIOLATED!" The door straight ahead was unmarked, but an iron bar at least two inches thick bisected it horizontally, held in U-shaped brackets firmly bolted to the brickwork.

It might well be a door opening to outside. Milo put an ear to it but could hear nothing. Removing the bar, he opened the door a crack, keeping shoulder and foot against it, just in case a wolf should try to come calling.

But stygian darkness lay beyond the door. Darkness and a powerful odor of cat. Milo closed the door and drew his saber, then opened it wide and quickly descended the two steps to the next level, lantern held above his head and eyes rapidly scanning the large, high room.

Chapter III

The Hunter tried to raise herself when the two-leg holding in his paw a small, white sun opened a part of the den wall and came in, but she was too weak to do more than growl.

Milo let his saber sag down from the guard position. The big cat was clearly as helpless as the kittens bunched behind her body. One foreleg was grotesquely swollen, obviously infected or abscessed; the other was torn, bleeding, and looked to be broken, as well.

There was a flicker of movement to his right, and he spun just in time to see the slavering jaws and smoldering eyes of a wolf's head emerge from a hole just above the floor. In two quick strides, he crossed the room and his well-honed saber blade swept up, then down, severing the wolf's neck cleanly.

But the headless, blood-spouting body still came forth from the hole, and as it tumbled to kick and twitch beside its still-grinning head, another head came into view, this one living and snarling at the man who faced him.

Milo thrust his point between the gaping jaws. Teeth snapped and splintered on the fine steel and the point grated briefly on bone, then sliced free. Milo jerked the steel out, but the dying wolf came with it, and behind him crouched another.

He split the skull of the third wolf, but even as its blood and brains oozed out, another was pushing the body out into the den.

"This," thought Milo, "could conceivably go on forever."

But as the lifeless fifth wolf was being slowly pushed through, Milo suddenly became aware of the rectangular regularity of the opening. Man-made! And men would surely have had a means of closing it.

And there it was! Half hidden in a camouflage of dust and dirt, a sliding door, set between metal runners on the wall above the opening. But did it still function?

In the precious moments between butchering wolves, Milo pulled and tugged at the door. Setting the lantern down, he drew his dirk with his left hand and used its point to dig bits of debris from out the grooves of the runners. Clenching the dirk between his teeth, he hung his full weight from the door handle . . . and it *moved*!

Another wolf, this time a huge, black beast. He chuckled to himself, thinking, "The Chinese used to say that you should never be cruel to a black dog that appeared at your door. Well, hell, I wasn't cruel to the bastard. I gave him a quicker, cleaner death than he'd have given me."

The black wolf had been in better flesh than most of his packmates, so it took the one behind a few seconds longer to push the jerking body out of the tunnel. And that few extra seconds' respite made all the difference. With all Milo's hundred eighty pounds suspended from it, the ancient door inched downward slowly, then, screeching like a banshee, faster. Finally, it slammed and latched itself in the very face of the next wolf, which yelped its surprise.

"Dik, Djim, the rest of you," Milo mindcalled, "take up the lantern, carry it as you saw me carry this one and be careful you don't drop it or strike it against something. Come the way I came." He opened his memory of the stairs and passages to them. "Be careful at the bottom of those stone stairs—a nest of rattlesnakes is denned on the floor there. Those with a taste for snakemeat can kill them. But any who want wolf steaks need only come in here and gut their choice of ten or twelve of them, fresh-killed. Oh, and there's water here too—I can hear it dripping."

Then an intensely powerful mindspeak drowned out any reply the Horseclansmen might have beamed. "What are you, two-legs? You carry a small sun in your hands, you slay many wolves to protect kittens not your own, you can open walls and close them, and you can speak the language of cats. *What are you?*"

The Hunter could no longer trust the witness of her eyes. At times they seemed clouded with a dark mist; at others she saw the images of three or four identical two-legs, and as many of the little, bright suns. Therefore, when first she sensed him beaming the silent language, she thought that others of her senses were awry as well. But at length, she beamed a question . . . and he answered her!

He just stood and stared at her for a moment, then, very slowly, he laid down his long, blood-dripping claw beside the little sun and took a few steps closer to her, extending one empty paw.

"You are badly hurt, Sister. Will you bite me if I try to help you?"

The sight of him faded into the dark mist, but his message still came into her mind. "Help this Cat? Why would you want to help this Cat? This Cat killed one of your pack last sun. Two-legs do not help Cats, they slay Cats, just as you slew those wolves."

He answered, "Wolves are enemies of us both, Sister. Besides, my brothers and I are hungry."

"You would eat *wolves*?" The repugnance in her thought-beam was clear.

He moved his head up and down for some reason. "Hunger can make any meat taste good, Sister."

All of the Hunter's life had been hard, and she could grasp the truth stated by this two-leg. Perhaps he then was truthful about wanting to help her. "If this Cat allows you to come close, what will you do, two-legs?"

"The bleeding of your right leg must be stopped, the wound cleaned and packed with healing herbs and wrapped with cloth . . . uh, something like soft skins . . . then the broken bones must be pulled straight and tied in place to heal. It will hurt, Sister, and you must promise to not bite us in your pain."

"Us?"

"Yes, Sister, one of my brothers must help me, he is skilled in caring for wounds and injuries." To himself, Milo thanked his lucky stars that chance had sent Fil Linsee with him. The young man was well on his way to becoming a first-rate horse-leech, and was certain to have a packet of herbs and salves and bandages somewhere on his person.

"Does your brother, too, speak the language of Cats?" the Hunter asked. She was feeling very strange, much weaker; it was now all she could do to keep her big head up.

The Hunter half-sensed an answer from the two-legs, but it was unclear. Suddenly, nothing was clear for her. The dark mist closed in, thicker and darker. A great waterfall seemed to be roaring about her. Then there was nothing.

As it was, Fil was the first man through the door, his long spear in one hand and the tails of a couple of thick-bodied, headless snakes writhing in the other. At the sight of the unconscious cat, he dropped his snakes and grasped his spear shaft in both hands, bringing the point to bear.

But Milo waved at the spear. "You won't need that, with luck, Fil. That cat can mindspeak. We were having quite a conversation before she passed out. We . . . you . . . are going to do what is necessary to heal up those forelegs. Do you think a cat will be much different from a horse?"

Fil came into the den and eyed the injured feline while keeping a safe distance from her, with his spear shaft between them. After sucking on his long lower lip for a while, he said, "Uncle Milo, that cat must weigh over two hundred pounds, for all she's not really well fed. That near foreleg will be tender as a boil, and it needs draining, which means cutting it in two, maybe three places. I value my life and my skin, Uncle Milo. I won't touch that cat unless she's well and firmly tied. She's bound to be too strong for even six warriors to hold for long."

Reflecting that the man was likely right, Milo thought hard. There was no rope in this party, and seven belts just wouldn't do this job. Maybe, he thought, behind one of those two locked doors . . . ?

A swift succession of short, heavy blows of the iron rod not only smashed the padlock but ripped loose the hasp as well. And Milo entered the door marked "FALLOUT SHELTER."

The room was a treasure trove—jerrycans of fuels, boxes of canned goods, several locked footlockers, a couple of axes, a long-handled spade, a pickaxe and a wrecking bar, all metal surfaces smeared with cosmolene and looking as if they had just been brought from the hardware store. The room was dry and there was almost no dust, as the door had been tight-fitting and weatherstripped, with a raised sill. There was an identical door in the opposite wall, but Milo postponed exploring what lay behind it, for what he now most needed was in the first footlocker he opened, several coils of strong manila rope, plus an assortment of buckle-fitted webbing straps.

Bearing their ropes and straps, Milo, Fil, Dik, and Djim filed into the den and bore down on the comatose cat. But suddenly there was a fearsome, if high-pitched, growl, and a kitten—probably weighing all of twenty-five pounds—stalked purposefully from behind his mother. Fur and whiskers bristling, ears folded back against his diminutive head, lips curled up off white little teeth, the kitten took his stand, tail swishing his anger and fierce resolve.

Milo received a silent warning: "Two-legs keep away from Mother or this cat kills!"

The other clansmen perceived the thought transmission as well, and stop they did, grinning and nodding admiration of such courage and reckless daring in defense of kin.

"Uncle Milo," said Dik soberly, "if that cub had two legs instead of four, I'd sponsor him to my chief. It's clear he's a Horseclansman born."

Handing his coil of rope to another, Milo slowly approached the little warrior. Squatting out of range of a pounce, he hoped, he mindspoke the hissing kitten. At the same time, on another level of his mind, he broadbeamed soothing assurance, having noticed that such worked with horses.

"How is my Cat-Brother called?"

The kitten did not alter his position, and he eyed Milo distrustfully. When he decided to answer, it was with open hostility. "This Cat is Killer-of-Two-Legs. Keep away or you all die!"

Dik slapped his thigh and guffawed. "Listen to him! What a warrior he'd be. Facing down four full-grown, armed men, and him but a cub."

Milo spoke aloud. "Don't underestimate him, Dik. Smaller than his mother, yes, but he's near as big as a full-grown bobcat, and I'll wager he could put some pretty furrows in your hide, if given the chance."

Then he added, "But we won't give him that chance, I hope. Two of you take off your jackets and hand me one, *sloowwly*, then get some of that rope ready. I could argue all day with this obstinate little bugger, and his mother will soon die without help."

With moving men to either side distracting his attention, Milo was able to flip the heavy coat over the kitten. And then it was a furious matter of grab and tussle, but finally, the raging, squalling little beastlet was securely wrapped in two thick leather garments and wrapped about with several yards of rope. The other two kittens had retreated into a far, dark corner.

First Fil cleaned the wolfbite and smeared it thickly with salve, then he adroitly set and splinted the broken leg, using part of his own embroidered shirt when he ran out of bandage cloths. But when he first began to shave the infected leg with the razor-keen skinning knife, the huge cat came to full and furious consciousness, straining at the ropes and straps pinioning her rear legs and fearsome jaws, growling between clenched teeth.

Milo tried to reach her mind, but it was useless. As well as he could, Fil went on about his shaving of the long fur.

As gently as possible, his sensitive fingers roved over the grossly swollen leg. He rubbed a portion of the discolored skin with a few drops of liquid from a small metal bottle, then dipped the short blade of a slender knife into the bottle.

At the first touch of the needle-pointed knife, the big cat squalled, and heaved her heavy body once, then unconsciousness claimed her once more.

Fil had the experience to keep clear, but the curious Djim caught the jet of foul greenish pus that erupted around the first thrust of the little knife full in his face. Cursing sulphurously, he stood up and headed for the water pool.

Fil opened a long gash and cut through to the bone, then pressed upon the leg until nothing but blood and clear serum flowed. He packed the open wound with dried herbs, smeared its gaping edges with salve and bandaged the limb with more of his shirt. After feeling the neck pulse to ascertain if his patient still lived, he gathered his instruments and trudged wearily toward the pool.

After the straining men had manhandled the limp form of the cat back to where she had been originally lying and had untied her rear legs, Fil Esmith took up the watch over his patient, squatting near her with the thrashing shape of a decapitated rattler before him, gobbling raw filets of snake as fast as his busy knife could skin, clean and slice them. Across the den, the red-haired Linsee twins were joking and chortling as they lugged bloody wolf carcasses up to the roof of the tower for skinning whenever the blizzard died down.

In one end of what had been the snake den, Djim Linsee squatted, kitten-sitting. Killer-of-Two-Legs had not been released, as he had hotly refused to tender his parole. The furious and frustrated little beast was managing to some-how roll his ropebound leather cocoon over and over from one side of the room to the other, alternately squalling for maternal assistance and beaming silent threats of dire and deadly retribution against every two-legs he had seen.

On the other hand, Djim had gained at least the condi-tional friendship and partial trust of the smaller and less pugnacious female kittens. The fuzzy little creatures were mindspeaking less and less guardedly as they avidly de-voured his lavish gifts of snakemeat.

Milo had found the inner door of the fallout shelter unlocked, though every crack had been sealed with wide strips of tape. Sealant removed, the door had opened easily to reveal a virtual efficiency apartment—two double-decker bunks, a chemical toilet, a two-burner petrol range, a stainless-steel sink with chrome pump in place of faucets, and a plethora of cabinets and drawers of various sizes and shapes covering every available inch of wall space.

After going through the contents of a few of the cabi-nets, some of the worry about their situation left Milo's mind. Even if the blizzard, now howling in full force, should last a month and the huge wolfpack should main-tain its siege until spring, he and the Horseclansmen would be well fed on the big sealed cans of powdered milk and eggs and orange concentrate, the stack upon high stack of freeze-dried foods still sealed in their plastic-lined foil pouches. There were jars of coffee (he tried but could not recall the last time he had tasted real coffee, though the nomads all drank certain bastard brews they invariably called ''coffee'') and sugar and jams, tins of tea, even a case of Jerez brandy, Año 72, plus a wide assortment of condiments and pickles.

Under one of the lower bunks was a flat steel chest, its lid padlocked and sealed with tape. The lock yielded to a few strokes of the iron bar. Within, the first thing that caught Milo's eyes was a finely tooled leather case about four feet long.

Nape hairs prickling, he lifted the case to the bunk and unsnapped its catches, then lifted the lid. Nestled on a bed of impregnated sheepskin lay a scope-sighted sporting rifle, blued barrel, chrome bolt handle and polished stock reflecting back the light of the lantern. Arrayed below the barrel were six brightly colored boxes, each labeled "REMINGTON .30-06 Sprgfld. 180 gr. pointed soft point 20 rounds."

With shaking hands, Milo lifted the beautiful weapon from its century-old bed and first lifted, then pulled the silvery bolt handle. The ancient Mauser action slid smoothly open and the ejector sent a bright brass dummy cartridge clattering across the room. The visible interior surfaces of the rifle gleamed as brightly as the exterior.

Milo slouched back against the cabinet behind him, a grim smile on his face. Six boxes, twenty rounds the box, one hundred and twenty cartridges, then; even if it took him a full box to reorient himself to a firearm and to zero this one in, he'd still have more than enough to seriously deplete the wolf population hereabouts, so they were only now trapped here until the weather improved.

But what about the cat? Even with the wolves dead or departed, she would be in a bad way. Unable to hunt for at least a month, she and those kittens would be white bones soon. True, he and the Horseclansmen could leave meat behind for her, but how long before it was all eaten or became inedible?

"Take them back with us? For the kittens, that would

work fine—strap one each on the backs of three men. But how in the devil do seven men get a two-hundred-and-some-pound injured cat down a bitch of an almost vertical hill, coated with ice and full of loose rocks?

"What we should do is just loll about here until the big cat is mended, then give her the choice of coming with us or staying here, but if I keep these men away that long, their clans will think they're all dead, and, likely, move the camp to a luckier place, probably in the very direction we won't go.

"Now if it only weren't for that damned hill, we could just build a sledge and—"

Fil's mindcall interrupted him. "Uncle Milo, the big cat is waking up."

When Milo strode into the den, Fil Esmith, and Bili and Bahb Linsee were watching the groggy beast, made clumsy by her bandaged forepaws, trying to get a hind claw under the strap still securing her jaws.

Milo moved to her side and squatted. Laying a hand on her head—he had long ago learned that physical contact always improved telepathic communication—he mindspoke her.

"Sister, I'll take the straps off. But you must promise not to tear off the little skins covering your legs with your teeth. Will you?"

The blizzard blew for three days, but the wind began to die during the third night, and morning brought a full blaze of sun in a blue sky. It also brought back the wolves, which had shrewdly left the exposed mesa during the blow. Bili and Bahb, who were atop the tower, working on the frozen carcasses with their skinning knives, mindcalled Milo as the first grey predators moved out across the frozen surface of the deep snow.

Carrying the cased rifle and a folded tarp, Milo climbed back up onto the tower roof. He had been classed an expert rifleman in both the armies with which he could remember having served, and during the long blizzard days he had read and reread the booklet that the Browning Arms Company had packed with the weapon, then stripped it, cleaned it and dry-fired it until he thought he knew all he could learn without putting a few live rounds through the mirror-bright bore.

Lacking the sandbags he recalled, he steadied the rifle on a tarp-covered dead and frozen wolf, opened the first box of cartridges and filled the magazine, then settled himself to wait until the maximum number of furry targets were in sight on the mesa.

The pack must not have found much if any game during the blizzard, for soon most of them were gathered about the tower, engaged in a snapping, snarling battle-royal over the skinned carcasses the Linsee boys dropped over as soon as the pelts were off. But a few wolves still were sitting or ambling at some distance from the tower, so Milo decided to sight in the rifle.

Far down, near the distant edge of the mesa, sat two wolves, intently observing something in the forest below. Milo centered the cross hairs of the scope on the nearer one's head and slowly squeezed off the first round.

The butt slammed his shoulder with a force and violence he had half forgotten. Below the tower, the wolfpack members were streaming off in every direction, yelping, howling, tails tucked between legs, looking back as they ran with wide and fear-filled eyes. But Milo did not notice, so intent was he on checking the performance of his rifle, which had thrown a good ten feet short of target and well to the left.

The two distant wolves had looked around at the noise, but as they had never been hunted with firearms, they failed to connect the noise with the small something that had drilled through the frozen crust, may not even have been aware of that small something, since it had arrived ahead of the noise.

Milo chambered a fresh round, then adjusted the scope and resettled himself behind it. The second round sizzled out of the barrel. Through the scope, Milo saw the target suddenly duck down, then shake his head and raise his muzzle skyward, looking about above him.

Again he adjusted the scope. The eighth round sent the target wolf leaping high in the air, to fall and lie jerking on the snow. The other wolf still was sniffing at his fallen packmate when a 180-grain softpoint ended his curiosity forever.

Milo had the tower top to himself for some time. The Linsee boys had descended the rickety stairs shaking their ringing heads and wondering how even Uncle Milo could stand those incredibly loud noises.

In a way, Milo felt sorry for the pack of merciless killers—they had no idea who or what was killing them. The loud reports kept them well away from the tower, which simply made it easier to shoot them with the long-range weapon. Milo tried hard to make each of his kills clean, and the tremendous shocking power of the mushrooming bullets helped. He never knew how many wolves got away, if any, but he stopped firing only when there were no more targets.

When he stood up finally and surveyed the slaughter he had wrought, he felt a little sick. Of all animals, he had always most admired wolves and the great cats. Sight of the tumbled, furry bodies and thought of the fierce vitality his skill had snuffed out so effortlessly pricked his conscience.

But the Horseclansmen did not share his anachronistic squeamishness, when once they filed out upon the roof and saw the windfall. Whooping, they lowered themselves down the walls and ran to the closest dead wolves, skinning knives out. Winter-wolf pelts were warm and valuable. They would become wealthy men at the next summer's tribe council, trading pelts for cattle, sheep, concubines and inanimate treasures.

By the fourth day after the blizzard had ended, the deer carcass was long since but gnawed bones and the snakes were curing skins; the cat and her kittens had lapped up almost all the powdered milk Milo had mixed and set before them, so he took Djim and Dik down into the forest to seek edible game.

Four big hares, however, had been all that the hunters had to show for over three hours' stalking when Djim's keen eyes picked out a large animal moving among the thick, snow-heavy brush. Alerted by mindspeak, Milo had raised the rifle and almost loosed off the round before the scope told him just what the animal was. Pursing his lips, he whistled the horse-call of the clans, and the chestnut mare broke off her browsing to come trotting out of the scrub.

Milo put out a hand toward the mare, but she shied away, going instead to Dik and nuzzling against his chest.

Smiling and patting the shaggy neck, he said, "Why, this is my hunter, Swiftwater, Uncle Milo. But I left her back with the other horses, in that deer park."

"Then it's a wonder she hasn't been wolf meat," commented Djim Linsee laconically. "I figure most of our horses are."

Dik hugged the mare's fine head to him. "Well, she won't have to fear that now. I'll take care of my good girl."

"Then we'll have to make you a tent down here in the woods," said Djim bluntly. " 'Cause it ain't no way you're going to get a horse up on that mesa, Dik."

Dik set his jaw stubbornly. "I'm not going to leave her alone down here."

Milo nodded. "No, you're not. You're going to fork her right now and ride back to the camp. Her fortuitous arrival changes the complexion of things. You've got your bow and your dirk." He unsnapped his saber. "Here, take this. Djim, give him your spear, too.

"Dik, Fil says that the big cat may never fully recover her strength in those forepaws. I'm going to persuade her to come back to camp with us, her and the kittens."

Neither Horseclansman evinced any surprise at the intent, for both had "chatted" often with the crippled cat, and Djim was now a virtual parent and frequent companion to all three kittens. To their minds, the cats were human, anatomical differences notwithstanding.

Milo continued, "Dik, tell the chiefs of all we have found and done here. Tell them to come with a large party, plenty of spare horses. We'll strip the ruin, up there, of anything we can use. Then, too," he grinned, "you won't want to leave any of your wolf pelts or snake hides behind. Tell the chiefs to hurry, Dik. Esmith and Linsee will be very wealthy clans by the time they leave this winter's camp."

"It'll take them at least a week to get around to getting here," thought Milo as he and Djim continued the hunt.

"They wouldn't be Horseclansmen if they didn't spend a couple of days and nights discussing the matter, then two or three more days arguing about how to divide booty that they don't yet have in camp. Then they'll take at least a day getting organized. Both chiefs and every warrior will insist upon coming, but in the end, half will stay behind to guard the camp and the herds.

"But maybe the week will give me time to read the rest of the records in that office. What I've found in there so far is damned interesting. Back-breeding then-living animals to produce extinct ones they were descended from wasn't then new, as I recall—the Europeans had reproduced a decent facsimile of the aurochs that way.

"And that could damn well be the origin of those cats, come to think of it. The only cats I ever heard of with fangs that long were called *sabertooth cats*, and they've been extinct in this hemisphere for ten, twenty thousand years. And those huge, long-horned bison, there're more of them around this part of the country than in any other place I can recall; they could easily have originated here."

"Uncle Milo," Djim mindcalled. "Elk dung, fresh, still hot!"

Shortly the two men came out of the forest into more open terrain. Well ahead, among the stumps verging a beaver pond, a solitary bull elk had cleared the deep blanket of snow from off the frozen ground and was pulling up bunches of sere grass. Raising his head with its wide-spreading rack of deadly tines, the beast gazed at the two men without apparent alarm. He had been hunted often by men and now realized that the quarter-mile of distance separating them was too far for the black sticks to travel.

A single shot of the antique hunting rifle dropped the half-ton animal, but Milo put another round into the head at close range as a precaution. Bull elk could be highly dangerous adversaries. Then he and Djim set about the skinning and butchering.

"The Hunter," thought Milo, "and her brood should be very happy with elk meat, and that's good. I want her in a damned jolly mood when I broach the subject of her and them leaving here for good and living with the clans. I think the idea of a steady, reliable, and effortless food supply will appeal to her, so that's one point in favor of my plan. For all her stubbornness, she's highly intelligent— more intelligent then even a dog or a pig, and they're supposed to be the most intelligent four-footed animals— and if you can convince her something's for her own welfare, she'll do what you say—as witness the fact that she hasn't pulled off her bandages once.

"If she's a sport, she's breeding true, because all three of her kittens can mindspeak, too. When she's better, she and I will have to travel around and see if we can find a mate for her, since she avers that there are more of her kind in this neck of the woods."

When they had arranged the choicer portions of meat into two weighty but manageable packloads, he and Djim dragged the hide, the rest of the meat, and the exceptionally fine antlers back to the nearest tall tree and hung them well out of reach of any but the smallest predators and scavengers to be picked up later. Then they set out for the ruin.

Thoroughly convinced of his own powers of persuasion, Milo chuckled to himself.

"Who knows—in time there may be yet another Horse-clan, a four-footed and furry one."

Chapter IV

James Bedford looked at the cover of the folder and frowned. Project *latifrons*. "It might excite some of them," he thought, "but it wasn't exactly what I had in mind when I took over. After all, what measure of charisma has an oversized, long-horned bison got, compared to a sabertooth cat or a weasellike creodont the size of a black bear? Hell, the Poles brought back the aurochs close to eighty years ago and the South Africans rebred themselves quaggas nearly five years back."

He sighed, leaned back in his chair, extended and crossed his legs, then closed his eyes, thinking. "I happen to know for a fact that Pearson's group in Alabama are getting all sorts of funding on their mammoth replication project. *That's* the kind of thing that grips the imagination, dammit! Why in hell can't I get the hard facts of life and funding across to Stekowski and Singh, to Harel and Marberg and the rest, why can't I?

"What we need are the kinds of projects they talked about when they first conned me into this operation, something that will grip the imaginations of the folks I have to impress. A ton or so of shaggy-haired moo-cow is just not in that category, unfortunately, and there is a fast-approaching limit to the amounts of my own bread I can plow into this without serious trouble.

"Furthermore, with the length of a bison's gestation period, it will be years before we can come up with anything worth showing or shouting about. But that ass Harel seems to be about as fond of predators of any kind as he is of bleeding piles, the Republican Party or inherited wealth. Hell, I guess it's fitting: a vegetarian who specializes in Bovidae. But he would be a whole lot easier to take, to work with, if he wasn't so damned arrogant, so critical of everyone else and so bloody sanctimonious about the fact that he doesn't eat meat.

"The longer I think on it, the more I'm coming to the certainty that this pack of multi-degreed con artists suckered me into this outfit for the sole purpose of milking me and my connections bone-dry. Executive director, huh? Ha! I have less real authority here than most of the hired help. The only time I'm made to feel at all important is when fresh inputs of money are needed."

Sitting up, Bedford switched on the voicewriter, made certain that the paper supply was adequate, refilled his mug with hot coffee, then began to speak.

"I'm just back from my latest fund-raising trip, which was a near-bust. Magori Hara, in Tokyo, avers that in the photos, the new calf looks most like the outcome of a Scottish Highland cow and a Tibetan yak than like any kind of bison, and I tend to agree.

"Uncle Taylor, in Washington, was raving over the progress of the Steakley Foundation, in Texas. Despite the failure of their glyptodont project, they have produced a capybara that weighs over two hundred kilos, he says, and replicated creodont types twice or more the size of the biggest living wolverine. He reminded me that Project *Patriofelis* was basically my idea and pointedly stated that he thought I should go back to where I was appreciated as something other than a money tree. He won't get us any more funding unless we come up with something a bit more colorful than Pleistocene bison, though.

"The New York types were cool, but polite, of course, and very evasive. Nor can I say that I blame them. This *latifrons* thing is at best lackluster, when compared to Alabama's mammoths and the great things the Steakley Foundation is accomplishing.

"In the replication-funding circles of Chicago and L.A., most of the interest seems to be in the O'Toole thing that's going down in Australia now. Their southern branch already is well on the way to a giant short-faced kangaroo *plus* a Pleistocene giant wombat that they say will be bigger than a tapir, almost rhino-sized. As if that weren't enough, their northern branch, in cooperation with the Indonesians, are going great guns on an accelerated-growth project designed to replicate the *Megalania*, a half-ton Komodo dragon.

"The only place I got any money was right in the lap, almost, of my previous affiliation. McLeod, in Fort Worth, gave me six million, though he made it abundantly clear that it was the last of his money we'd see unless we embarked on a more promising project.

"I knew better than to even try Houston or Atlanta, eyebrow-deep as they both are in Alabamian mammoths. And all you can hear in any part of Florida is the six or seven accelerated-growth projects set to produce ten-meter alligators and caimans for the leather trade; they've already got a few twenty-footers, I saw some of them last year. Grim. Jaws nearly a meter and a half long. If only the accelerated growth processes worked on mammals as well as they do on reptiles. . . .

"Now, I have to go in, call a staff conference and break the bad news to Dr. Stekowski and the rest of his jolly crew that, with very strict budgeting, we might have a year of life left here, unless the damned dumb *latifrons* thing is shoved onto a back burner and we start in cooking up some project with more popular appeal. I'm going to strongly recommend one more time that we take advantage of the pair of snow leopards we've been offered, acquire such other Felidae as we can get quickly and cheaply, then get at it at flank speed, while still we have the wherewithal to operate at all. A donnybrook with Dr. Harel is dead certain, and this time around I just may deck the son of a bitch, for I have little to lose, here and now. This place is doomed unless it changes fast, and the Steakley folks are itching to have me back, anyway, Uncle Taylor says."

Bedford pressed the buttons for "Print," "Separate" and then "Laminate." When the machine had disgorged the completed page, he inserted it in his ongoing binder of personal files, then switched off the machine and made ready to leave his sanctum sanctorum for the main building of the complex. Dr. Harel and certain others never ceased to twit him about keeping private records in addition to those filed in the computers, but he liked things he could if necessary read and check back on without the power required for activating said computer or one of its outlets.

"So that the sly, conniving sonofabitch could spy on me, pry into my notes the way he does into everyone else's around here, that's the real but unstated reason Harel wants me to give over my voicewriter records. No less than three times I've come back from trips to find that earnest attempts had been made to pick or force the locks on this office and the private storage room, down here on this level.

"Why, oh, why won't Stekowski and Singh and Marberg back me in getting rid of Harel, forcing him to resign, get out? They clearly have little use for the bastard, either. All I can figure is that he has something on them, collectively or individually. There can be no other reason why such accomplished professionals would just supinely let the arrogant ass walk all over them the way he does. Then again, maybe it's just the fact that he's pushy, openly aggressive, and none of the rest of them are . . . well, not so much so, so overtly so, anyway."

At the top of the steep concrete stairs, Bedford opened a plain steel-sheathed door and entered a short corridor. He reflected that no matter how much Harel might bitch about the primitiveness and isolation of the place, they could have done far worse in obtaining—for what amounted to almost nothing—the lease to the facility and the surrounding land.

It had first been built in the fifties or early sixties to house some super-hush-hush project of the federal government—one large and three small chambers cut out of the living rock of the plateau, with only the stair head, what was now the corridor in which he stood and a broad, stubby masonry tower aboveground, all of these spaces at one time filled with equipment of some nature, the traces of it still remaining.

When the army or air force or whoever had moved out in the seventies or eighties, then the state had moved in and erected a tall tower of steel to straddle the one of masonry and provide a firewatch facility. A succession of earth tremors had finally brought that metal tower down, and by the time Bedford first had been shown it, the plateau and all had been deserted, though sealed and fenced and with a plethora of no-trespassing signs bearing impressive warnings.

Of course, it was state land and could not be sold; however, a thirty-year lease had come very cheaply and the state had even replaced and strengthened the access road, which had been rendered impassable in the last, strongest of the earth tremors.

What had passed into Bedford's group's possession had been only the nucleus of the present facility, however—the underground rooms (the largest of which the state had turned into a garage, with a ramped entrance), alcoves filled with lockers at the foot and head of the stairs, the present hallway (which then had been the entrance foyer) and the two tiny chambers within the short, squat masonry tower; the plateau had been bounded at its edges with an eight-foot Cyclone fence topped with razor wire, there had been a concrete helipad with wiry grass growing up between its joints, and the wreck of the downed fire tower stretched its length of rusting metal just where it had fallen some years before. Off to one side, now all overgrown with many years' worth of vines and weeds, had been a long, sprawling jumble of never-used bricks which had been trucked in by the federal owners just before they had abandoned the site for good, their presence forming an enduring example of the boondoggle and lack of foresight of the long-ago administration of President James Earl Carter, to James Bedford's way of thinking.

After he had brought in a seismic expert to examine the land and give the professional opinion that it was no more geologically unstable than any other part of the range, the preceding ruinous jolts having been at most a fluke and most unlikely to recur within hundreds of years, after the access road had been rendered once more sound and usable, after he had obtained detailed plans of the newly completed Steakley facility, he had contacted one of the family-owned businesses: a general construction contractor.

By the time Stekowski, Singh, Harel and the others actually saw the plateau—having flown from their temporary location in Colorado to the nearest airport and coptered from there—the crash-scheduled project was nearing completion. The only one of the group who had not seemed pleased was Dr. Harel. The big, burly man had snorted and sneered, jabbing and pounding on objects with his blackthorn walking stick for emphasis until the gangling, slow-to-anger engineer and the tough, feisty construction superintendent had seemed on the point of physical assault. In times since, Bedford had often reflected that it might have been best for all concerned had he allowed—nay, encouraged—the two to beat Dr. Harel into a state of bloody insensibility; such an experience might have taken out of the man a measure of the pigheaded arrogance and the dogged insistence on the constant having of his own way no matter the cost, which would have saved Bedford not a little trouble and the project a good deal of money in the time since.

Based on the preliminary plans that had been formulated during the courses of his series of conferences with the group of scientists, Bedford had had the onetime garage level enlarged and enclosed, then had solicited the advice of experts on the housing of big cats and fitted the space out in accordance with their years of experience and ideas.

But on the very first full conference after they had begun to actually occupy the premises, Dr. Harel had rudely dashed Bedford's planning in that direction. "Why in the world did you not consult with *me* before you wasted our money in such a way, *Mr*. Bedford? I could have told you that there will not be, will never be, any scrap of research done here into reproduction or replication of any stripe of dirty, bloodthirsty predator beast. No, it has been decided by us scientists that we will undertake to replicate the *Bison latifrons* of the North American Pleistocene.''

Only by painful exercise of will had Bedford bitten down a hot reply that day. To the burly, shaggy, bearish, overbearing man he had said, coolly, ''For your information, Dr. Harel, the actual funds pledged this project have not yet come through. Therefore, all of the cost incurred at this site and during my fund-raising travels I have paid out of my own pocket.''

''Now, that is true, selfless generosity, my boy.'' Stekowski had spoken feelingly. ''Of course, when the funding materializes, you will certainly be repaid every last penny, and—''

''Do not presume to speak for the group, you old fool,'' snarled Harel, subjecting Stekowski to a glare hot enough to melt basalt. ''We have agreed that only I now own that power here, you may recall. Besides''—he turned to Bedford with a cold, hostile smile—''wealthy as the Bedfords are with monies ground out of generations of poor working-class laborers, I am certain that whatever sums he has here expended are to him as pocket change would be to such as us.''

For the umpteenth time, James Bedford mentally castigated himself. ''I should've bashed the bastard there and then, that very day, hour and minute, then resigned and gone back to the Steakley Foundation. But, of course, I didn't, I took it. I took it for the sake of Stekowski and Singh and those others I had come to know and like before that damned opinionated Harel suddenly appeared on the scene and bulled and bullied his way to where he was virtual dictator of the project.

"But now . . . ? Hell, if the project doesn't change course and that damned quickly, there won't be any more funding, and that means that there'll be no project. Odd— sometimes something in the back of my mind tells me that that's just what Harel wants, too, that that's precisely where he's been heading all along, for whatever cryptic reason."

He frowned. "And that's just what's so crazy about this notion of mine, too: Harel's no big, well-known name in this field—why, I'd never even heard of him, I don't think; if this project does go down the drain, he'll be out in the cold, too, and with far less chance to snag a position elsewhere than people of the professional renown and stature of Stekowski or Singh or some of the others. So what could possibly be his reason for wanting to sink this venture? Creeping insanity? No, he rants and raves and swings his damned cane and, sometimes, throws things at people, but I'm dead certain that he does so fully rationally, for purposes of shock and the intimidation effect on his erstwhile colleagues; he's a thoroughgoing bully and behaves like one.

"Could he be deliberately putting us on the skids to benefit a supposedly former employer's project? It doesn't seem likely. Dr. Stekowski says Harel was last connected with the dwarf fauna thing that Britain, Israel and Greece are collaborating in on Cyprus and Crete—hippopotami, elephants, that sort of thing—and God knows Stekowski's original felid project could've posed no slightest threat to them or their goals. Oh, sure, there could've been dwarf forms of smilodon and the related types, but none have ever been found in fossil form. Indeed, the closest thing to a dwarf of this kind was just recently pried out of a glacier in the Canadian Rockies—a strange beast, looking much like the *Homotherium*, but smaller, more lightly built, and with digitigrade rather than plantigrade hind feet, *Panthera feethami*, they're calling it. Dr. Stekowski told me, away back when before the advent of Harel, that he had access to some genetic material from this find. It was this that he was basing the original project on.

"The Canadians tried replication, of course. Hell, that project may still be going on. But they've never reported much success, and Drs. Stekowski and Singh think they know why; their ideas make more sense than anything else I've heard about it all.

"Apparently disregarding the size of the find and certain other factors, they've been trying for a full-fledged, over-sized, classic sabertooth cat, big as or larger than an African lion, and a damned hefty lion, at that.

"Dr. Stekowski says that as this beast was found in a montane glacier, we can safely infer that it resided and hunted and bred in mountains which—as the body showed certain cold-weather adaptations—were probably as cold as or colder than they are at the present time. He goes on to say that mountain-living species seldom become really large, as compared to their lowland cousins. The find was about as big as a largish leopard, though somewhat heavier than a true leopard, more the build of a jaguar or an undersize, gracile lion.

"Therefore, his idea sounded like a good one, one that had a more than just fair chance of working, of producing replication of the *Panthera feethami*, or at least something halfway between true replication and mere reproduction. And I was not the only one impressed, either, not by a long shot; I was able to round up some really good, very sizable funding from hither and yon, on the basis of his ideas, his and Dr. Singh's.

"Dammit, it would still work! It must work, and soon, or I'll be back down in Texas, out a fat chunk of my own money, and all the others here will be preparing résumés . . . and all thanks to one loutish ass of a hector brattishly insistent upon always having his own way."

He found the conference room empty, of course, but took his place at one end of the table and keyed the intercom to reach all work and housing areas of the complex before saying, "This is James Bedford. Would Drs. Stekowski, Singh, Marberg, Baronian and Harel please join me in the conference room as soon as possible. An urgent matter must be discussed immediately."

Ruth Marberg was the first to arrive. Seeing her puttering about the coffeemaker in her stained lab coat, slacks and stout brogans, with her mostly grey hair pulled back in a tight bun at the back of her head, Bedford thought of the razor-keen intellect and the sometimes frightening degrees of efficiency that her grandmotherly, usually-placid demeanor masked.

The coffee started, and she came to take her usual place at the table and after looking hard at Bedford, shook her head. "Jimmy, Jimmy, you're still not taking proper care of yourself. I can see and so too could anyone with even one quarter of a functioning eye, too. You press yourself too hard, you don't rest enough, sleep enough, eat enough. Certainly, this project is of importance, but it is not so earthshaking as you should break your health over it."

When he opened his mouth to reply, she raised a stained, work-roughened hand and went on, "I know, I know, as Beanbreath Harel is always telling me, I am only a 'mere

veterinarian,' not a most exalted medical doctor. But Jimmy,
Homo sapiens sapiens is just another animal, you know,
and flesh and blood and bone are still and always flesh and
blood and bone and resistant to only just so much deliberate abuse and overusage.

"If you won't sleep and rest more, at least eat more.
Come to my rooms, upstairs, eh? Despite old Beanbreath
and Clifton Singh and their efforts at enforced conversion
to vegetarianism, I still make and treat myself to chicken
soup and cabbage rolls and even—dare I to breathe such
predation?—the occasional steak or chop or piece of liver.
Landislas sometimes joins me, and Zeppy Baronian used
to, before Harel and Singh started working on her mind
full-time. Do come up and dine with me, Jimmy. I promise to not try to seduce you to anything but my cooking."

At that moment, the door opened again to admit a
balding but quite distinguished-looking man of roughly the
same age as Ruth Marberg. He limped a bit; his progress to
his chair was assisted by another woman, younger than
Ruth, with wavy blue-black hair, light-olive complexion
and a figure trim and attractive for all its wide hips and full
breasts.

Both Bedford and Dr. Marberg arose, and while she
moved down the room toward the older man, Bedford
asked, "What in the world happened, Dr. Stekowski? Did
you fall? Are you badly hurt? Should I call for a chopper
to get you down to a hospital?"

The grey-haired man held up a slightly trembling hand,
but spoke in a strong voice. "No, no, James, I'm all right,
really, I just twisted my ankle . . . I think. I'm ill accustomed to running over rough ground, I fear." He smiled
wanly, paused, then added, "It might've been much worse,
of course. Dr. Baronian, here, really and truly saved my

life out there. You all must promise to help shield her from the wrath of Dr. Harel.''

''Well, what in hell did happen, Dr. Stekowski?'' demanded Bedford. ''And why is Dr. Baronian going to be in need of protection from Dr. Harel?''

''Because he's certain to be somewhat less than happy when he finds out that I put down one of his precious Russian wisents,'' replied Dr. Baronian, matter-of-factly. ''But I had no option. It was either kill that cow or watch her kill Dr. Stekowski.''

Bedford reflected that he had thought he had heard, despite the thick soundproofing layers of the complex walls, the sound of a gunshot, but he had of course just assumed it to be one of the state hunters in the forest below the plateau clearing out excess elk.

''You mean to try to tell me, Doctor, that you put paid to a full-grown wisent cow with a single shot? You must admit it's hard to believe—they take a lot of killing. Where did you come by a rifle, anyway?''

Zepur Baronian smiled. ''My rifle is up in my room, where I was myself when I heard the commotion down below. I've never loaded and fired so quickly, I don't believe. But then I was granted a perfect target; the cow was coming at Dr. Stekowski, head lowered, so all I had to do was place my shot precisely where the spine joined the skull. And I did just that—my father taught me well.''

''Look,'' said Bedford, ''how did this all come about? The last I saw, as I came in here today, those wisents were fenced into the far-western enclosure. How the hell did one manage to get out? Have they learned to open the gate? I doubt that even one of them could knock down any of that fencing, not with every single post sunk and cemented the way they are.''

Stekowski sighed and shook his head, the fluorescents glinting on his scalp. "It was all my fault, I'm afraid. There were many other things I would've been better off doing, but I was curious to take a look at the calves, so I took one of the runabouts, the three-wheeler, and drove out to the far enclosure. I know, I know, I should've taken one of the silent, electric ones, but the gauges on both of them indicate that they needed recharging and I just did not want to wait for them to charge and—"

"Well, why the hell weren't they, or at least one of them, charged?" demanded Bedford. "Have their batteries gone bad on us?"

"Most unlikely," answered Ruth Marberg, "it was all the fault of our dear *Führer*. He can never be bothered with cleaning up after himself or even going to the vast trouble of plugging in the recharger plug after he's used those ATVs. That's what he uses all of us *Untermenschen* around here for."

"Now, Ruth, dear," Stekowski gently rebuked, "that is not at all fair."

"No, Landislas," she snapped testily, "but it's all true, nonetheless. That despicable, detestable man considers all of us to be nothing more or less than his personal servants, his lackeys, his . . . his *Spucknapfen*, his *Knechten*! I have endured much of him, far more than ever I would have but that you seemed to wish that he—rather than you or our Jimmy, here, as would have been more of a rightness—rule in all things. But now that his misbehavior has nearly cost your life . . . your so very precious life . . ."

"Ruth, Ruth," said Stekowski placatingly, "it truly was my own fault, not that of Dr. Harel, really."

Dr. Marberg's face reddened and she opened her mouth to retort, but Bedford spoke first. "Hey, hey, let's talk this out later, huh? I still want to know just what happened out there, how that wisent cow got loose and why Dr. Baronian had to put her down.''

''So,'' said Stekowski, ''I drove out and let myself into the far enclosure with the three cows and the two calves. The older of the calves, the bull calf, has started to graze already and his horn buds are quite pronounced. But I guess I got too close to them to please the cows, for they began to get most protective of the calves and to make threatening movements in my direction, so I decided to leave them in peace. Followed at a distance by that biggest cow, the barren one, I drove back to the gate, unlatched it and drove through, then closed it and, I thought, latched it again. But I must've not done it properly, for I had but just driven some few yards in this direction, it seemed, when I heard it swing back open and heard that big cow bellow, then start to gallop after me.

''It was then that I set the machine to maximum speed and made for the complex. I was within only a few yards of the side parking lot when the engine sputtered a few times, then ceased to function, and before I could even think of what to do next, the cow was upon me, had charged the machine from the side and knocked it over. I was shaken up a bit, of course, but the cage had held and I was not hurt, really. Not so with the machine, however; something in the rear compartment had commenced to spark and to smoke, and so, though I knew that if I remained in the cage I would most likely be safe from the loose cow, I decided to try to run the few yards to the parking lot, thinking that if all else failed, then I could clamber into the bed of Juan's truck for refuge.

''But I had only run a short way when I twisted my ankle, fell and could not again arise. The cow, which had trotted off a distance after having knocked the three-wheeler over, had apparently seen me emerge and was in pursuit. It seemed that I could actually feel her hot breath upon me. I was terrified. Then came that booming rifle crack and the cow fell in her tracks as if she had been poleaxed.

"Dr. Baronian had but just helped me into the building when we heard your summons to meet you here. You were away a long while, this time. Did you experience some difficulty, perhaps?"

"More than just some difficulty, Dr. Stekowski," sighed Bedford, then asked, "But where's His Highness, Dr. Harel, pray tell? I'd not like having to go through all this twice."

"Probably still in converse with his Russian buddy," replied Zepur Baronian. "He wheeled the videophone into his office about an hour or so back and double-locked the door."

Bedford felt the heat as his face and neck suffused with his boiling blood. His voice came out under tight control. "*Harel has been on a satellite hookup to Russia for over an hour, this time? At one hundred and fifteen dollars and fifty-five cents per minute?* He doesn't hear very well, does he? Well, I'll bring this to a screeching halt. You folks wait here. I'll be back."

From the window of the corridor, he saw the still, shaggy mound of the wisent carcass near the edge of the side parking lot. The black buzzards were already circling lower and lower over it. On a sudden impulse, he deliberately bypassed the door to Harel's office and made his way all the way back, to the shop area. There he found the two men for whom he was searching.

Juan Vivás stood, meticulously wiping clean, then racking each tool in its proper place, while Joe Skywalker scattered compound chips on the concrete floor to absorb spilled fluids. Joe was the first to see Bedford enter the workplace, and he straightened with a warm smile—white teeth flashing against his dark, scarred face.

"Good to see you back again, Mr. Bedford, sir. Me and Juan, we just this minute finished fixing up that snowblower, and while we was at it, we tuned up the engine of the tractor, too. Won't be no trouble now this winter coming like it was last spring."

The squat, broad man turned from the tool rack. Since his own, dark face was considerably broader, so too was his smile. "¡*Jefe*! *Bienvenido*! Do you hunger? Please to allow me the time to wash and I will prepare whatever you may wish, but . . ." A doleful look came over his features then, and he went on to say, sadly, "No meat is to be found, alas—fresh, frozen, freeze-dried nor even tinned. Of a night last week, the two so-distinguished and *muy loco* doctors, they searched my kitchen and the larders and even went into the cold place and cast everything of meat over the side of the mesa. Then they forbade me or Joe or anyone else to ever bring up any meat or fowl of any kind again, saying that did we so do our jobs would be the cost."

"Forget anything that Harel and Singh said, Juan, Joe," said Bedford. "Remember, you two work for *me*, not for them. But that aside for the moment, I'm glad the tractor is back in shape. There's a freshly killed wisent cow lying out by the side lot; she got out and attacked Dr. Stekowski, and Dr. Baronian shot her from her room window, upstairs. I want you two to take the tractor, drag the carcass to where you can work easiest and then skin, clean, and butcher it. You ever dress out a full-grown buffalo, Joe?"

Looking from beneath his brows with a slight smile, the

man replied, "Not legally, Mr. Bedford. License for buffalo hunting in these parts costs more'n I used to make in a month, most times. But, yessir, I have been at a few buffaloes, over the years. Good eating. 'Specially the tongues and the livers and the hump ribs."

"Fine." Bedford nodded. "When you two get the carcass butchered and hung to age in the coldhouse, Juan can come back to the kitchen and slice the liver and make up a big meal of it fried with lots of onions, mashed potatoes, gravy, the works. Cook enough for Drs. Stekowski, Marberg and me, possibly Dr. Baronian, and you two, of course. We can have the tongue tomorrow, then start on the hump ribs. Okay?"

Showing every gold inlay in a grin that seemed to stretch literally from ear to ear, Juan nodded. "It will most assuredly be done, *Jefe*."

"Uhh, Mr. Bedford, sir . . . ?" Joe Skywalker asked, diffidently. "Uhh, please sir, do you want the robe and the head and all?"

Bedford chuckled. "Hardly, Joe. If you do, you take them with my blessings, unless Juan fancies some or all of them, in which case you two will just have to draw straws or cards or roll dice for them, I guess. Now get to it, you two, before those buzzards get to it first."

Proceeding back up the hallway from the shop areas, Bedford halted before the door of Harel's office, rattled the knob, then knocked. When there was no whisper of a response, he rapped harder, at last pounding with the side of his clenched fist at the firmly locked portal, while shouting at it, "Damn you, Dr. Harel, get off that phone."

After waiting a few more moments in silence, he nodded grimly to himself and spun on his heel to stride purposefully back up the hallway, past the conference room, to the entry foyer. From a box set in the wall, he took a key and unlocked the door marked "KEEP OUT! HIGH VOLTAGE! DANGER!"

Once within the ground-floor room at the base of the brick tower, Bedford knew exactly what to pull, exactly where it was located on the wall. He had been there when it was first installed and had asked lots of questions of the installers; now he was very glad he had done so.

Relocking the door behind him, he went back to the conference room to await the now-certain arrival of Dr. Harel.

Nor did they have long to wait. Bedford had but just filled a cup with fresh coffee and sugared and stirred it when the door crashed open and an obviously thoroughly enraged Dr. Harel stomped in, blackthorn stick in hand.

"Mr. Bedford," he snapped peremptorily, "that videophone is defective. You must obtain us a new one, immediately. I was in the midst of a most important conversation with Dr. Piotr Ivanov, in Beloretsk. Suddenly, *poof*, the screen was black and no sound, nor would the stupid American-Japanese abortion respond to any more commands. Order a Russian-made videophone this time; true, they are not so smooth and sleek and fancy, but they are always and completely reliable. Well, do you hear my orders, Mr. Bedford?"

"Perfectly, Dr. Harel. I doubt not but that you were heard as far away as Boise," James Bedford replied, shoving aside his cup and arising from his chair. "But as for ordering any new v-phone, much less one of those cast-iron clunkers the Russians turn out, it will not be necessary, not necessary at all. By the way, just how long did you and your Russian friend chat this time?"

Harel sneered and sniffed. "That information is none of your affair, Mr. Bedford; you own no need to know it."

"On the contrary, Dr. Harel," snapped Bedford, "at one hundred and fifteen dollars and fifty-five cents the minute for that kind of hookup to that part of the world at this time of day on a v-phone, it is very much my business to know just how much your irresponsible long-windedness has cost us this time around. After all, it is I who am trying desperately to keep this project afloat financially, and with damn-all cooperation from you, sir. I'm told you'd been on that phone for at least an hour—over nine thousand dollars' worth, including taxes, Dr. Harel!—and after you refused to respond to my knocks on your office door, I simply went into the tower and disconnected the v-phone cable. Furthermore, the next time I catch you in such a wastrel act of selfishness, I'll do it again! We are going to be on a very tight budget here for the next year or so, thanks to your dumb, lackluster *latifrons* project. The only way I could beg any money at all was to promise that we'd drop the ongoing project and start something with more appeal."

"Such as . . . ?" grated Harel, his big hand gripping the stick as if it were a sword, gripping it so hard that his knuckles shone out white as new-fallen snow. "Or need I ask at all, *Mr.* Bedford?"

"Such as," answered Bedford with not a little satisfaction in the words, "a project aimed at replication of *Panthera feethami* or something similar to it, Dr. Harel. I can get real, large-scale funding if we work on such a project for the next year and I can take out tangible proof of a reasonable amount of progress on it."

His broad, big-featured face become a livid purple, his thick lips skinned back to show his large teeth, Harel swept his stick up above his head and brought its length crashing down on the table, roaring, "*Never*! Do you hear me? Never! Never will anyone here do such a thing! No flesh-eater of any description will be replicated or reproduced in my project here!" He punctuated each short shout with yet another slamming of the length of his stick on the tabletop.

Coolly, Bedford said, when Harel had paused for breath, "When you've finished this tantrum, Dr. Harel, we can then perhaps carry on a civilized and reasonably civil discussion, eh? For there are no available options, you see; no one will fund Project *Latifrons* any further. I gave at least one tug to every possibility and no approach produced anything, the—"

"*Tantrum?*" growled Harel. "I'll show you who is your master for good and all, you impudent capitalist pig!" So saying, he whirled the stick of dense, tough wood up above his head yet again, but this time it was clearly not aimed at the table.

That blow never fell, however. Thinking, "Goddammit, enough is enough! No way is that fat fucker going to beat me with that cane," Bedford gave the threatening man his left fist with all his force behind it squarely in the solar plexus.

With a wheezing grunt, Harel doubled, gasping. The raised stick dropped from his fingers and both hands sought the place that hurt, covered it.

Fists cocked and ready, should more force be needed, Bedford half crouched on the balls of his feet. Stekowski just sat and stared, looking as stunned as Harel; the old man had paled, and although his lips moved, no sound emerged from them. Between them, Ruth Marberg and Zepur Baronian took Harel's elbows and got him into a chair, the elder woman then picking up the blackthorn stick and tucking it out of sight behind the coffee console.

Gradually, the adrenaline began to drain from Bedford and he was able to ask in almost-normal tones, "Where the hell is Dr. Singh, anyway?"

Dr. Baronian shrugged. "Probably in his quarters, upstairs, meditating. He turns everything off when he meditates, the intercom, included. Want me to see if I can find him, Jim?"

He nodded. "Yes, if you would be so kind. I'd really like to have us all in here when I tell the full story of this last trip and lay out what we are going to have to do to survive, to get as much as one more dollar of funding."

They all sat down to wait for Drs. Singh and Baronian to come. Bedford stirred absently at his cooling coffee and kept a wary eye on the big man, who had begun to breathe more easily. Bedford sensed that unlike many bullies, there was beneath all the bluster and the histrionics a potential for real and dangerous violence.

(*"If only I had known there and then just how right my intuition concerning Dr. Harel truly was,"* he later was to record in his journal, *"how different things might have been for us all. Who was it who said that 'if only' are the saddest words in the English language? They are."*)

Chapter V

Bundled against the chill of the concrete-walled underground room, Milo spent long days reading the notes of James Bedford by the light of the smaller of the gasoline lanterns. It was well that they had killed and helped to bring back the big bull elk, for the night following that fortuitous kill saw another blizzard blow up, this one lasting in fits and starts for the best part of a week, and Milo could only hope against hope that his lone rider had found a secure place to hole up with his mare until it blew itself out and he could once more proceed on his mission to bring the clans back here to these ruins.

As he continued to read through the boxes of folders, all meticulously arranged by date, he came to understand the long-dead James Bedford, came to sympathize, to empathize with the man, came to feel that he had truly known him. He regretted that Arabella Lindsay had not lived to this day, for she too could have read the journals and would have been truly delighted to do so, for they and what they contained would have answered so very many of her questions about the world of the dead past, partially quenched her endless curiosity about the people of that world of her forebears and how they had lived.

"Hmm," he thought. "How old would Bella be today were she alive? About mid-sixties, I think, not a really great age for clansfolk. Yes, but not more than a barehandful of that first generation of the people from the MacEvedy Station are still alive, either—the change from settled farming and animal husbandry to a constantly moving existence of herding, hunting and gathering was just more than any but the very toughest-fibered of them could take and live on. Even so, they lived on longer as new-made nomads than they could, any of them, have expected to subsist at that doomed station, with or without being perpetually besieged by plains rovers, as they were when the clans and I chanced across them.

"But the children and grandchildren of those first-generation Lindsays and MacConochies and Dundases and Hamiltons and Rosses, MacKensies, Douglases and Keiths, born to the life, are become the tough, self-reliant and hardy clansfolk of today. And a large proportion of them possess at least a fair amount of telepathic ability, too, which makes a survival trait for such a life as we all lead, so in the course of succeeding generations it should become stronger and more prevalent among the Horseclansfolk."

While musing, Milo had stuffed his greenstone pipe with some of the fine tobacco out of one of the sealed tins that had been a part of James Bedford's survival store. That done to his critical satisfaction, he used one of the butane lighters Bedford had also included to light the mixture, drawing in several mouthfuls of the smooth, fragrant smoke before thinking on.

"In a way, it's too bad that the late James Bedford's

mind didn't run to fiction writing, for he owned a rare talent to put the reader directly into the places and situations he describes here in this journal of his; he could no doubt have made quite a name for himself as an author in that long-ago world. But if he had, of course, this place most likely would not have been here when we needed it and that huge wolfpack would probably have torn us all to gobbets and eaten us . . . and I don't think that even my unusual constitution could've survived that sort of death.

"Even so, Bella would've been enthralled to read this journal, for it would've answered so many of her questions about the world as it was so long ago. She never ceased to be obviously thrilled to hear of how, before everything went to hell, thousands of folks every day were transported across the widths of whole continents or oceans in the space of less than a day, flying high above the clouds—six and seven miles straight up—sitting in complete comfort, watching moving pictures, listening to music, eating, drinking, sleeping, talking with others, reading books or magazines or newspapers, whatever they wished to do at the time.

"She knew well of ground vehicles, both tracked and wheeled ones, of course. Unlike most inhabited places, the MacEvedy Experimental Agricultural Station had managed by hook or by crook to keep some of its vehicles and sophisticated firearms, and even its electricity was in operation and use up until only a score of years before her birth. But she did not know of the networks of fine, wide, paved roads that once connected tens of thousands of towns and cities one with the other, and it excited her to hear of how vehicles not too much different from the stripped hulks scattered around the MacEvedy Station could, on those roads, cover in an hour or less distances that would now exhaust a good rider with a string of remounts to travel in a full day.

"And she never tired of having me open my mind, my memories, that she might see through my eyes the vast multitudes of people who inhabited that world, the differing races and nationalities. She especially loved to go into my memories of the cities—the larger ones in particular, New York, Tokyo, Mexico City, Rio de Janeiro, Rome, Paris, Los Angeles, Chicago, Hong Kong, Singapore, New Delhi, Cairo, London. And such a sojourn was always followed by hundreds of questions about anything and everything having to do with the people and their everyday lives, their artifacts, their habits, the huge buildings, where they raised their crops, what kinds of livestock they husbanded. One image which she never had ceased to ask him to recall was that of flying into the Los Angeles area one night, one Santa Ana–cleared night, with the tens of thousands of lights below the plane stretching from horizon to far horizon like a vast swarm of fireflies.

"She was just born a century or so too late," Milo sighed to himself, puffing on his pipe and filling the low-ceilinged, icy room with layer on layer of blue-gray smoke. "Poor little Bella, she hungered for any slightest scrap of new knowledge concerning the past, that dead world of her ancestors. And I really could impart her very little of the scenes she most craved, traveling as I did mostly from one war to another, generally in the more primitive parts of the world where my services were needed, going mostly by air, at that—and there's damn-all to be seen from six or seven miles up, unfortunately—and one almost never encounters ladies of fashion in swamps, jungles, mountains, deserts, the bushlands or montane forests where I spent the bulk of my time after the U.S. Army decided I was too old and retired me.

"Hell, by their lights, I *was* too old. I enlisted in 1938—or was it 1937?—and I think my age was listed then as thirty. Yes, I looked older, looked just as I do now, in fact, but the army of that time, between World War One and World War Two, could not afford to be at all picky or to pry too deeply into an otherwise healthy, acceptable and qualified would-be recruit's past, not in an era when the most they could pay privates was twenty dollars a month and found. But even so, by the early seventies, the Pentagon records indicated that I was pushing sixty-five, pushing it damned hard, too. And the damned whiz kids who had managed to fuck up a war we could've easily won in the beginning went into screaming tizzies at the mere thought of a sixty-four-year-old lieutenant colonel leading a combat unit in Vietnam."

He chuckled evilly in remembrance of the half-disbelieving type who had at last physically confronted him in a Pentagon office, so long ago, his narrow, bureaucratic mind almost blown by the utter, patent impossibilities of the unimpeachable documentations and the mid-thirtyish-looking officer who sat beside his desk, the left breast of that officer's blouse solid with row upon row upon row of campaign ribbons and awards from three wars and several nations besides his own.

Milo had just shrugged. "Mr. Henshaw, I cannot help it if I did not age as you feel I should have. You Pentagon hotshots may well control a lot of things in this sad, screwed-up world, but the will of God is not one of them, thankfully. You have my personnel file and all of the other DOD records, all of the fingerprints match—including the new set you had me impress today, right? So I am in fact

Lieutenant Colonel Moray, Milo, no middle initial, 0-2-284-755. Right? Right!"

The paunchy, jowly man just stared at Milo for a long minute. Despite the air conditioning, sweat gleamed on his balding head; his short, pudgy fingers trembled and his dark, beady eyes blinked incessantly behind the thick lenses of his horn-rimmed glasses. All through their several meetings, his color had alternated between a pasty white and a glowing beet red. His thin lips fluttered, and Milo suspected that the anus bunkered up between those porcine haunches must be spasming wildly.

At last, the most uncivil civil servant burst out, repeating himself for the umpteenth time, "But . . . but you simply *cannot be* Lieutenant Colonel Milo Moray. I don't know who or what you are, but you absolutely cannot be *him*! It's impossible, do you hear me? The doctors at Walter Reed say that you have the physical constitution of a *twenty*-five-year-old man, did you know that, whoever you are? And Lieutenant Colonel Milo Moray is almost *sixty*-five years old, and you . . . you don't look one day over *thirty*-five years old, if that! So who are you? What are you? When did you assume Moray's identity and why?

"Yes, your prints match the records . . . but that can only mean that someone, sometime, somewhere, has doctored them, and that's a job for the CID, I think."

"Then why don't you ring CID up, Mr. Henshaw?" Milo said disgustedly. "And while you and they are playing your games, just let me get back to 'Nam, to do what I do best."

Pale once more, Henshaw again stared at Milo. "You must be a raving lunatic, whatever else you are. You *want* to go back to that filthy, bloodsoaked hellhole? Anyone with any sense or the moral fiber to recognize that what we are doing, have done, there is wrong is doing everything possible, pulling every string pullable, to get out, get reassigned to almost anywhere. It's a no-win situation, and the plug will certainly be pulled on the whole stinking imperialistic mess just as soon as Senator McGovern is elected president and that warmongering Nixon is out of Washington.''

Milo smiled coldly. ''Mr. Henshaw, were I you, I would not make the error of holding my breath until the senator becomes president. Despite everything that you believe, disbelieve and opine, I am a good bit older than you, I've been around America and Americans some longer, and I can tell you that they are a proud people, a people accustomed to winning, and very damned few of them are thus likely to vote for a man whose plan is to crawl on his knees to Hanoi, to plead abjectly for peace with a savage, barbaric enemy, a catspaw of international Communism.

''But whether we eventually surrender to the type of people that McGovern represents, run out on our friends or not, so long as we're still fighting, I want to be there; so either retire me from the army or cut me orders back to 'Nam. I'm tired of farting around here with left-liberal defeatists—'Lose the world without killing anybody'—like you, too many members of Congress, most of the media and the unwashed, unshorn packs of young Marxists who seem to show up at the sight of a television crew, with their beads and flowers and narcotics and not enough brains inside their craniums to tan the hide of a pygmy shrew.

''Yes, this war has ground on for far too long, our citizens are getting tired of it all, tired of getting young men back in coffins, tired of living with the gut knowledge that once more, just as in the Korean War, American arms and aims have been stymied, stabbed in the back, betrayed, by a rotten combination of hubris, fuzzy thinking and cowardice—if not outright treason!—on the parts of their elected leaders, legislators and appointees.

"I don't like to think that perhaps my onetime commander in chief was a willing pawn of the Communists, a man with no strength of convictions, dimwitted or just a pitiful coward, so I often in my own mind attribute Harry Truman's successful efforts to see the Korean War lost to his preoccupation with things he no doubt felt were more important to him, the nation and the world, things such as coming up with choice gems of barrackroom filth and invective to sling at anyone who failed to appreciate as exalted art the caterwauling his daughter called singing.

"Hard on the heels of his disgraceful display of gutlessness, the Bay of Pigs fiasco, in Cuba, John Kennedy proceeded to commit us, to plunge us arse-deep into propping up the Diem regime in Saigon. French shilly-shallying, on-again-off-again governmental support of their hard-fighting troops in Indochina had already resulted in a humiliating defeat and loss of the north to Ho Chi Minh and his cadre of Marxist stooges, the splitting up of the country and the turning over of the non-Communist south to Diem and his criminal family with their hordes of equally criminal sycophants.

"Now, true, Mr. Henshaw, John Kennedy had had nothing whatsoever to do with the installation of Diem; that had been done by the French colonials and their figurehead-puppet emperor. But if our then commander in chief had had the intestinal fortitude to—even as late as 'sixty-two, when he had heard General Taylor's report—insist that as part of the price for an increased American presence and aid commitment, either Diem do things our way or be replaced by someone who would, he might have lived long enough to see a victory in Vietnam; and even if not, he at the very least would've seen more real possibility of victory than there was when he was assassinated barely three weeks after his coreligionist, Diem, had been deposed and shot.

"As before, Mr. Henshaw, as with Truman, I dislike having to think that Kennedy and Johnson after him were tools of international Communism, despite the clear indications of either that or such degrees of naiveté and stupidity as to boggle the mind. Therefore, in their particular cases, I usually assume that they both were sufficiently preoccupied with active domestic socialization of this once-great nation of ours as to not really care to devote much of their personal time to Southeast Asia and to just allow the Pentagon whiz kids to run their costly, bloody and unforgivable little games with the lives of thousands, to drag the war out for needless years and so devastate much of what had been some of the richest, most productive land anywhere upon the Euro-Asian landmass that they now have to *im*port food of every sort."

Henshaw's lips were become a thin, compressed line and there was now depthless hostility in his eyes. "Moray, what you've said here in the last few minutes smacks to me of nothing less than flagrant insubordination if not outright treason! I now can see and thoroughly understand why your records show such flattering notes and commendations from that fascist, reactionary, Russian-baiting, right-wing radical fool Barstow. You're just like him. Joe McCarthy would have loved you with your groundless accusations against three of your avowed commanders in chief!"

A smile flitted briefly across Milo's face. "Why, thank you, Mr. Henshaw, thank you very much."

Henshaw sat for a moment with his mouth agape, his face a very picture of puzzlement. "For what, Moray?"

Milo bedded the hook with secret delight. "Why, for those compliments, of course, Mr. Henshaw, those completely unexpected but still deeply appreciated compliments."

Henshaw's face went from red to ashen once more, and a hint of fear came into his eyes. "Moray . . . colonel, are . . . are you quite well?"

Milo chuckled. "If anyone should know, it's you, sir. If you're in doubt, why not read through Walter Reed's report on me again? Or you could ring them up, for that matter. If what you are actually questioning is my mental and emotional condition, then, no, I am not mad . . . but consider this: even if I were and knew it, I'd be expected to give you that same answer. Right?

"As to why I thanked you, what I found complimentary was your comparison of me to Eustace Barstow."

"But . . . but . . . how . . . what . . . ?" spluttered Henshaw, his pale face and hairless head slowly edging again from pink to pinker. "That man is certifiable! How he's retained so much power for as long as he has is simply beyond me or any other rational person. He's—"

"He's a true patriot, in his own way," put in Milo quietly. "He was one of the first men to have recognized the true and deadly danger to this nation, its people, all free nations of the world and even civilization itself that was then and is still poised by 'our brave Russian ally' of World War Two. If I and others had paid more attention to him, worked for him and with him, away back when, instead of doing our own version of the Wanna-Go-Home Boogie, there is at least a slim chance that we and 'Nam and the rest of this suffering world wouldn't be in the sad shape it is today.

"I know full well that what you said was in no way intended as flattery. Nonetheless, Mr. Henshaw, I took it and take it as just that. And not the least of my reasons is this: anyone who so fervently supports Senator McGovern's candidacy as you seem to do is patently well beyond mere liberalism and into true leftist thinking and beliefs, and when a leftist of any water calls me such things as right-wing radical, reactionary and fascist, then I am comforted in the knowledge that I have impressed upon him the true facts that I fundamentally oppose him and everything—every rotten, red thing—for which he stands.

"You questioned Eustace Barstow's retention of power. Well, I cannot but wonder just how and when a thing like you managed to secure a place in this, the nerve center of our nation's military establishment . . . and I mean to find out, too, Mr. Henshaw. Perhaps I should seek out Eustace Barstow and ask him about you, eh? You have any idea where he is just now, Mr. Henshaw? No? Then why don't we ring up Langley? Surely the CIA would be able to put us in touch, don't you think?"

Pale still again, Henshaw hissed, "You were well advised to leave well enough alone, Moray. I have influence in more places and levels than you could ever imagine. I've been a government employee for almost twelve years now, and my loyalty has never once been questioned, *by anyone*. The last I heard, this is still a free country, and that means that I have a right to my opinions, political and otherwise, whether you or Barstow or any other of your stripe of Neo-Nazi warmongers approve of them or not.

"I mean to see you out of our army as expeditiously as possible. You'll never go back to the war zone, understand? And that will be all to the common good—one less bloodthirsty killer there.

"Now you get up and get out of my office this instant! The smell of death is on you and I want you out of here. Now, get out!"

The best part of four days were required to get Milo in touch with Eustace Barstow. He had about given up, in fact, and was sipping a drink while watching the late news on the television set in his hotel room when the telephone jangled.

"Moray here," he answered.

"I understand you've been looking all over D.C. for me, Milo," said his caller. "Okay, I'm in the Shoreham lobby, so heave out the broads and I'll come on up there, bearing bottle, good stuff, direct from the Danish Embassy. You have a bucket of ice up there? Good."

Save for a close-cropped head of snow-white hair and a few more wrinkles, the Eustace Barstow who presently appeared at the door to Milo's hotel room was not significantly different from the Major Barstow to whom he had reported at Fort Holabird thirty-odd years before, the Colonel Barstow to whom he had reported in Munich or the Brigadier General Barstow for whom he had briefly worked while World War Two wound down and ground to a halt. It had been most of nine years after that before he had again run into Eustace Barstow. Just back from the stalemate in Korea but not at all sure that he wanted to become again the wealthy, privileged, globe-trotting man of leisure he had been prior to that mishandled war, Milo had agreed to serve Barstow's operation on a strictly one-time-only basis.

After the backslapping, handshaking and exchange of

friendly obscene insults, the white-haired man in the meticulously tailored silk-and-cashmere suit carelessly tossed his fedora onto the bed and handed Milo the padded-suede bottle pouch.

When he had unzipped the pouch and lifted out the liter-size bottle of clear liquid, he remonstrated, "Great God, General, *akvavit*? Why don't you just drink grain alcohol? One's about as strong and deadly as the other."

Barstow chuckled good-naturedly. "Because I'm queer for caraway, Milo. Kümmel is good for the digestion—both the Germans and all the Scandinavians swear to it as fact. Use lots of ice, Milo, it's best when it's as cold as you can get it."

When they had ritually touched glasses, Barstow threw down the three or four ounces of hundred-plus-proof liquor in a gulp before Milo had hardly sipped his own.

As he refilled his guest's extended glass, Milo shook his head and asked, "How often do you have to be sent to Reed or Bethesda to dry out, General? Or is there a classified facility for men of your rank and status?"

Barstow chuckled again. "You know, I'd almost forgotten just how goddam insultingly insubordinate you can be at times, Milo. That endearing trait of yours is directly responsible, as you well know, for the fact that with almost thirty-five years—including your four years of reserve time—of service and three wars behind you, you're still only a lousy light colonel. You were ordered out, to be sent stateside, no less than six times that I know of in the last ten years; hell, man, if you'd come when ordered, you'd most likely have two or three stars by now. Why didn't you?"

Milo half smiled. "Would you believe me if I told you

there was just no way I could've gotten out when the various orders reached me?''

''Hell, no!'' snorted Barstow. ''Any man who managed to get out of Dien Bien Phu and clear down to Saigon, through the length of a country swarming with Vietminh, and did it all alone and unaided, without even a fucking guide and showed up without a scratch on him, could get back to Saigon again. So why didn't you, damn you? The truth, this time, please.''

''Okay, General,'' Milo said. ''I didn't come out because not only was I needed where I was, but I knew that what I was doing there was damned important. In D.C. or wherever, I'd've been put to shuffling papers, playing politics at O-club parties, expected to suck up to congressmen and perform similar useless, senseless functions. Not to mention being expected to lie to everybody and his brother about how well that war we've now lost was going.

''General, what the hell is the point in committing an army to a war it's not going to be allowed to fight properly and win? God in heaven, we didn't even need to commit ground troops, not away back when. We owned the capability to subject the northern ports and population centers and larger supply points to high-altitude precision bombing just as we had German and Jap targets in World War Two; before they ever got a tenth of their air defenses set up, we could easily have turned Hanoi into a second Dresden, Haiphong into another Hamburg. You know it and I know it: the only thing the Reds of any nationality and race respect is pure, raw force; if we'd hurt them bad enough at the outset and shown a resolve to keep on hurting them, to annihilate them if necessary, they'd've cried uncle goddam quick, left the south alone, at least given a public appearance of living up to the Geneva Accords. So why didn't we do it, huh?"

With an enraged snarl, Barstow hurled his glass of ice cubes at the side wall. "Oh, damn you, Milo! Don't you think we tried to get that very order? Not just me, but quite a few others, some whose names would no doubt surprise you, men who you wouldn't expect to be willing to advise and consent to that kind of totally destructive warfare. God knows, *I* was shocked to the core to find out they were on our side in the matter. But Johnson seemed to be firmly under the control of the fucking whiz kids, seemed to be abso-fucking-lutely convinced that left alone to do it all their way, they'd shortly present miracles, and of course all they ever produced was worse than zilch—destruction, all right, and on a massive scale, but generally in all the wrong places, and a war that has now dragged on for so long that not a few domestic onetime supporters are beginning to sound more and more like the fucking pro-Communist agitators.

"And naturally, when Johnson finally came around to our way of thinking, got it through his head at last that the so-called brain boys he'd inherited from Kennedy had either snookered him and the country or had been just blowing wind all along, it was too late in the game, way too late for anything short of a nuclear strike, and even in the extremes to which he'd been driven by events, he knew better than to order that."

"It just might've been just what the doctor ordered, General," stated Milo grimly. "That way, we wouldn't even have needed to risk planes and crews, just delivered the load by missile."

Barstow shook his head. "Milo, you've spent a whole hell of a lot of time out of the country, and so I doubt seriously that you're aware of some facts. One of them is this: a whole lot of people in the U.S. of A. are scared absolutely shitless of doing any frigging thing that conceivably might upset the fucking Russians enough for them to throw *their* nukes at *us*, and not all of these people are in any way, shape or form the least bit pink, not that our own native crop of Marxist traitors don't use that lever and any other they can lay hands on to discombobulate their fellow citizens, retard our war effort—such as it's been— and speed the Communist conquest of Southeast Asia.

"If Johnson or anyone else in a position of power had seriously proposed even a small-scale, surgical strike against North Vietnam with nukes, oh, Lordy, there would've erupted such a shitstorm that it would have had to be seen and heard and endured to be believed. Even if some rabid, leftist member of the defeatist press hadn't had it leaked to him by a fellow traveler in the DOD or the White House, you can bet your bloody arse that one or more of our pack of Commie-lovers in the legislative branch would've had it in the papers and on the air in nothing flat. I tell you, Milo, certain elements of the news media have proven themselves of more value to the Reds in this war than five or ten full divisions of the NVA. To hear or to read the shit put out by those scaremongers, the whole damned country is in a state of constant turmoil and all of our allies are appalled at what we're doing in and to Vietnam and are turning away from us in droves, as consequence. In the holy name of First Amendment rights, these bastards are cynically betraying their own, native land to the fucking Commies.

"The newspapers would be bad enough, Milo, but the fucking TV is a goddam monster. You remember the old blood-and-guts training films we used to use? The ones that had fucking trainees fainting and puking their guts out? Well, compared to the footage the fucking networks are broadcasting all over America right at suppertime these days, those training films would be about as shocking as any damned Disney cartoon would be, anymore.''

Milo's visitor sighed gustily and shook his head forcefully. ''Lordy, Lordy, how I do carry on. Build me another drink, will you. My tirades always leave me dry as the Mojave. But I'm not the only one who blows off on occasion and calls spades fucking shovels, am I, Milo?''

Milo looked at Barstow quizzically for a moment, then abruptly nodded. ''You heard about me telling off that peckerhead over at the Pentagon, huh? Tell me, how in the hell did something like Henshaw get to an apparent position of some power over there, anyway?''

Barstow's lips twisted in a moue of disgust. ''Oh, hell, Milo, you ought to've guessed that already—he and a whole pisspot more just like him came in at the start of the Kennedy administration. But you guessed right on the power—he's been there more than eleven years, assiduously kissing asses and, more likely than not, sucking carefully selected cocks as well, and not just in the Pentagon, either. He's managed to acquire a goodly collection of ears, which means that your performance at his office the other day has wedged your scrotum into a crack, my friend.''

Barstow grinned. ''Not that I don't like whatall you told the bastard. I couldn't've said it better myself.'' He chuckled. ''I liked it so well, in fact, that I played that tape over three times, Milo.''

''Henshaw *recorded* our, ahhh . . . conversation, then, General?'' demanded Milo.

Taking a drink from his new glass, Barstow waved his

hand, then lowered the glass from his lips and shook his head. "No, no, no, Milo, Henshaw doesn't even know a tape was made. Some of my people made it . . . well, people who work ostensibly for someone else, but also for me, actually—wheels within wheels within other wheels, if you get my drift."

Milo recalled the almost identical expression spoken by Barstow almost thirty years before, in Munich. "Just like all your earlier operations, General?"

This time the visitor laughed and nodded, smiling broadly. "*Mais oui, mon vieux!* Deception has always been my stock in trade, it's what gives value to my services . . . which don't, any of them, come at all cheaply. I'm shrewd and as devious as old hell, but I'm an honest man, too, I never yet have failed to give value for value. And that dictum applies to both employers *and* employees, Milo."

Milo sighed. "Am I about to hear yet another recruitment pitch, General?"

"Not really, no." Barstow set down his glass of ice and gazed over steepled fingers at his host. "After all, what is there that I could offer you for service to me, eh? Money? Hell, you're richer than old Croesus ever dreamed of being, right now. Rank? If you'd cared at all about that, you'd've played ball with the army these last ten or so years; besides, few of us are or are known to be military personnel, anyway—you recall that surely from the work you were so kind as to do for me in Indochina, back in 'fifty-four. And in that regard, Milo, I still feel that I owe you a bundle for that, so tell me, my old friend, what can *we* do for *you*?"

Seeing the old pain in Barstow's eyes, sensing the humility of guilt in his voice, Milo put iron into his own words. "Stop it now, General. I'll tell you now just what I told you eighteen years ago: Martine's—my wife's—death was *not your fault*, not in any way your fault. Understand? Like many another innocent before and since, she was just in the wrong place at the wrong time and those circumstances conspired to kill her.''

"But, Milo," said Barstow, "it was *me* who persuaded you to go on leave from the army and take passage to Saigon as a tourist, as just a seemingly ordinary tourist, dammit.''

Milo nodded once. "Yes, and you said not a word about Martine going along with me. That was purely *her* decision. I tried to talk her out of the notion, to dissuade her, several times over. But she retorted that as I'd been away at war for over three years, she deserved and meant to have at least the next three years of my time. What could I say after that? So she went with me, thrilled to be again in a French-speaking city, among Frenchmen and their families, military folks, who knew her family of old.'' He paused, then went on, "Even had I had the heart to stop her, I doubt that I could've done so other than physically, at that point.''

Barstow shook his head. "Maybe, maybe not, Milo, but *I* could have done it, very easily . . . and I'll always regret that I didn't, it will always be one of the crosses I must bear to my very grave. No." He raised his hand once more. "Let me finish, tell it all, you've the right to know just how I used the situation, used her, to what I then thought my and your advantage, damn me for the cold, callous, calculating fool that I was.

"Look, of all people back then, I knew just how unstable, how volatile, how deadly dangerous was the situation in Cochin and Tonkin at that time, especially for anyone who might be considered to be or taken for a Frenchman or Frenchwoman, particularly one in any way connected with their military or governmental establishment.

"It was risky enough to send you, but some risk had to be taken, just then, to achieve my ends, get the information needed, and I knew you and knew that if anyone could take care of himself in a sticky situation, it was you.

"When Martine chose to accompany you, I decided that she would provide deeper cover for you. Anyone—man or woman, friend or complete stranger, Caucasian or Oriental—could tell when you two were together just how much of love and caring one for the other was in your relationship, so how could it then be even so much as suspected that you were anything more than what you were supposed to appear—a wealthy American couple spending some time as the guests of certain French people in Saigon? Had I taken the time to think, had I only taken that little bit of extra time to think it out as deeply as I should've . . ."

"Look, General," said Milo earnestly, "think now, think back on it, huh? Martine was killed, yes, but not by intent. Daphne, Madame Cler, she was the target of that bomb, it was her car that they rigged, and we never knew for certain just who did it, either. Yes, it could've been, might've been, the Vietminh, but it just as well might've been any of half a dozen aggregations of racketeers—Asian *or* French—for not only the Minh had it in for Daphne's husband and her brother. It doesn't take much sophisticated skill to wire a bomb to the ignition of an automobile, only access to wire and primers and explosives, all of which were in abundant supply all over Saigon at that time, hell, still are and will continue to be into the foreseeable future."

Barstow grimaced. "Until the Cong come in and take over Saigon, of course," he said bitterly, adding, "Which scenario seems to be nothing less than exactly what Mc-Govern, Church and the rest of that flock of pinkish doves want to see. They'll gladly let the rest of the world go Communist or go to hell, just so long as they can be free to legislate this country into a fucking Swedish-style socialist welfare state, completing the work of Roosevelt, Truman, Kennedy and Johnson.

"That McGovern!" He spat in disgust. "He swears he's going to, if elected, give one thousand dollars to every man, woman and child in this whole frigging country, just because they're here and alive, apparently. What he doesn't think about or talk about is where the fuck he's going to lay hands on the two hundred plus billions it's going to take, not to even make mention of the four or five billions more that the fucking bureaucrats will gobble up in the distribution. I tell you, Milo, the Democratic candidate—or, more likely, whoever is telling him what to say, what to promise—has a cranium stuffed with top-quality fertilizer, fresh from the horse.

"But since we're back on the subject of shit, you're deep in it, my friend, so far as the Pentagon is concerned. They're no longer at all accustomed to truth-saying and honesty over there, you see, and they're therefore scared to death of anyone who is capable of speaking out bald facts and, more, of anyone who does so. Your encounter with Henshaw rattled not a few cages, and the intent is to make you pay dearly for such temerity, such unbridled honesty. But I just may be able to pull you out . . . with your cooperation, of course. Will you cooperate, Milo?"

Chapter VI

In the dank little underground room, James Bedford's sometime private office, now lit brightly by a gasoline lantern as ancient as the other artifacts cluttering the space, Milo set his eyes once more to the laminated pages of Bedford's personal journal.

"I'm beginning to suspect unplumbed depths to Dr. Harel," he read. "His behavior, all of what I thought to be mere bluff and impressive bluster performed for simple shock effect, may well be in truth that of a really violent, incipiently dangerous man. So, although I've left the v-phone cable disconnected for the nonce, I've just placed some calls on my private, scrambled line to some folks back east; I want to know more about Harel, a great deal more, and in as much detail as possible. If his tantrums are not as deliberate as I thought, are really more or less uncontrollable, then we'd best—for our own safety—get him the hell out of here."

The next page in the binder began: "Just spoke with contacts in re the snow leopards. Cheers! They're still available to me and this project. I've arranged, moreover, to trade the surviving bull and cow wisents for them—even trade, no cash involved, which will certainly help us here, under the circumstances. I've put Juan and Joe to preparing a place for them and such other cats as we might later acquire or breed.

"Everyone seems exhilarated over the prospect of changing our project over into another direction . . . everyone except Harel, of course. The man is always either sullen and completely uncommunicative or livid, shouting, beating on inanimate objects, throwing things and stamping his big feet. When I refused to reconnect the v-phone at his order, he proceeded to go into a towering rage and smash and batter the set into so much plastic and metal junk, roaring that if he couldn't use it, no one would. He's used the regular phone, though, to place several late-night calls of some duration to Russia, to his buddy, Piotr. Those calls weren't scrambled, but as they were conducted in some dialect that no one here seems to understand, they didn't need to be. After each succeeding call he's been more hostile.

"Singh, on the other hand, is ecstatic, there's no other word to adequately describe him and his demeanor since we decided to override Harel's *Latifrons* obsession and go back to Stekowski and Singh's original Project *Feethami*. He and Stekowski have been on the phone to Canada, among other places, and have been assured that the genetic material will be here any day now. they've also gotten word of the capture of one of the exceedingly rare white, mountain jaguars and have been heating up the lines between here and South America trying to get either her or genetic material from her.

"Nor is Singh the only one. I've never seen this place throbbing with so much life, such intense purpose. Dr. Marberg has found us a replacement for Harel, too, an old friend of hers, a German, a Dr. Wilhelm Müller, who worked on both the *Panthera spelaea* project in Greece *and* the *Thylacoleo* project in Australia. Old as he is, and he's quite a few years Stekowski's senior, such a man still will be invaluable to this project. His in-depth knowledge of and vast experience with the very species we are attempting replication and eventual reproduction of should speed up our success, and, strapped as we now are, every day saved is precious.

"Once we get close enough to even apply for an international patent, of course, we'll be out of the woods, every investor and his maiden aunt will be clawing each other for an opportunity to put money into the project and we'll be as rich as the mammoth project down in Alabama or the creodont project in Texas. But until that happy day, we're going to be on a tight, an exceedingly tight, budget, even if I plow every available cent of my own year's income into our project.

"But back to Harel. I want the loud, arrogant bastard out of the project altogether and off this plateau. If my investigators come up with information to indicate that he's not dangerous to people he works with, maybe I can get him a slot in that new project down in Southern California, that dwarf mammoth thing—surely he'd be happy with that, and he does seem to know his stuff professionally, so he would certainly be valuable to them.

"I'd still like to know just how he so quickly buffaloed Singh and Stekowski and, later, Baronian; maybe the investigations will shed some light on that little matter, too. All of his available records certainly appear to be in order, but then, skillful, well-funded experts can forge just about any document needed by anyone for any purpose . . . though I cannot for the life of me figure out just why anyone would want to sidetrack so innocuous a project as was Singh and Stekowski's original one.

"Now if some other foundation or government was racing us for completion of a *Panthera feethami* replication or a closely related project . . . ? But, hell, the Canadian government project was put into abeyance, wasn't it? And they're the only ones I know of who were even trying, who had the necessary genetic material to try . . . Wait just one goddam minute, here! The fucking Russians!

"Harel and his damned Russian bunghole-buddy, this Piotr, the dude who got us those wisents hard on the heels of Harel getting the project headed his way. Could it be? Could it be that darling Piotr and his colleagues are themselves working on a sabertooth or dirktooth replication? Or could it be that they have even somehow 'acquired' by hook or by crook *feethami* genetic material? Could Harel be a Russian himself? He speaks Russian languages well enough, true, but according to his records, he was born and reared and educated in Israel. So we come back to the possibility of forged records, again.

"If anyone is capable of such forgeries, it would certainly be the Russians. But they wouldn't, I think, be doing it for the money—more likely, for the prestige, the international acclaim, the damned propaganda value to them, still trying to prove socialist science the superior of western, capitalist science, just another rendition of the same old tune.

"But if Harel *is* a Russian, why is he so openly contemptuous of all things western? One would think that he would cover his true beliefs thoroughly, in order to not be even suspected of . . . But of course, God, I'm dumb, at times! He's supposed to be an Israeli Communist, this fact covers his close contacts with Piotr and the other Russians he's always phoning and praising and bragging of knowing intimately. Clever, clever, Dr. Harel . . . or whatever your real name is.

"Now, next question: Should I phone these suppositions to the investigators? No, no, I think I'll just let them work on unraveling the loose ends they already have in hand and see if they come to the same conclusions. After all, I could very well be wrong on this matter; God knows, I make my full, honest share of mistakes in life."

Milo kept suppressing the urge to skip ahead through the boxes of binders and see whether or not Bedford's conclusions regarding Dr. Harel had been proved correct in the end. The man Bedford described sounded to Milo like a type who would definitely benefit from application of a prolonged knuckle massage about the regions of the head and torso. He recalled that such men had been much more common in that long-ago world where few persons went armed than in this present one wherein everyone did so. Who had it been who averred back then that an armed society must be perforce a polite society?

"Most of the societal problems, back then, in the more or less civilized portions of the so-called western world, were directly caused by the lofty but totally incorrect premise that all persons are created completely equal," the ageless man mused, while puffing in vain at his cold pipe.

"I've always been dead certain that what that group of rebels, revolutionaries, eighteenth-century radicals really meant when they framed those words was that all free, white, Anglo-Saxon gentlemen were created equal . . . and they were wrong, even at that. No two men or women are ever exactly, precisely equal in any meaningful ways, never have been, never will be.

"Some are physically stronger, some weaker, some are

taller, some shorter, some are smarter, some denser, some are faster, some slower, that's just Nature's—or, if you will, God's—way of it all. Some are gutless wonders, some are brave, some are very good, decent, honorable, some are bad and incredibly vicious, and the only provably sovereign ways to protect the good from the bad are very forceful and often fatal.

"The mistake of many of the western nations of the decades just preceding the horrendous eclipse of their era and the dawn of this present one was in allowing far too much power to the rather fuzzy-brained sociologists and experimental psychologists; given entire populations to play with, they and their ivory-tower supporters wreaked hellish havoc, turned beautiful, populous cities into places more deadly and dangerous than any jungle could ever have been.

"They and their minions first virtually disarmed the law-abiding segments of those populations with restrictive laws in regard to the private possession and use of fire-arms, then virtually tied the hands of the various strata of law-enforcement persons, insofar as apprehension and treatment of real criminals was concerned, so that in the end the only people who could live and work or play in any degree of physical safety were either those rich enough to afford private bodyguards or those willing to or scared enough to break the gun laws and carry deadly force.

"The so-called social scientists could never seem to get it through their pointy heads that some people are just born bad. No, they continued to prate about all criminality being 'society's fault,' no matter how heinous or despicable the crime, no matter how arrogant, unrepentant or recidivistic the perpetrator.

"Those self-proclaimed 'saviors of mankind' wreaked

an inordinate amount of mischief with their crackpot theories and out-and-out wrecked a proportion of real civilization, and I am very glad to say that in the end, none of the bastards survived. There are none of them and their hare-brained disciplines extant in this world; folks here live by might and by right and mostly are too busy wresting out enough to eat to spend much time scheming against others."

His gaze alighting again upon the already-read stack of Bedford's folders, Milo thought, "Although I spent damn little time in the country after the early seventies, I still did a lot of reading of U.S. newspapers and periodicals, whenever and wherever I could lay hands to them, so I recall more than just a little of these replication and recreating projects, the vast sums of money that went into them, the chaotic brouhahas that preceded and surrounded some of them and the final decisions that allowed nations and groups and companies to actually patent recreations of extinct animals. As I remember, though, the antislavery factions still were squabbling about the issue of whether or not primates with enhanced mentalities could be patented right up to the end of everything, and naturally, certain religious groups fought the entire concept from the outset on the shaky grounds that if God had had the animals die out, then it were blasphemous to try to bring them back to life . . . not that very many people paid all that much real attention to the foaming fanatics on that or any other subject.

"And God knows, the religious and quasi-religious flakes had as many *causes* over the years as the left-liberal flakes, the right-wing radicals or any of the rest of the lunatic fringe. After a short while, a reader got to recognize the telltale catchwords and phrases that indicated 'this was written by or for a bunch of flakes' and most of us would just glance briefly over the patent claptrap or skip it entirely.

"Thinking back on Bedford's thing, the whole business seems to have started back between World War One and World War Two, when the Poles or Hungarians or one of the other Slavic peoples of Central Europe got it into their heads to breed back various strains of domestic cattle to reproduce the aurochs, *Bos primegenus* I think the scientists called it, the European wild ox that was the supposed ancestor of all domestic cattle and had been extinct then for about three centuries. They succeeded, and that gave everyone big ideas, but half a century or more went by before much more was done.

"Then, in the seventies, the Russians, I believe it was, started trying to back-breed to produce the extinct European wild horse, and at almost the same time, some privately funded group in Texas set out to try to back-breed to the Pleistocene wild horse of North America. Then, in the eighties, DNA and gene-splicing were brought into the picture, followed by other advanced procedures.

"Meanwhile, the Japanese had funded secretly a research project designed to produce reptilian hides for luxury leathers faster than Nature could manage, and that project spawned the processes of artificially stimulating growth. The replicators cheered and leaped to apply the process to their various projects, only to find that no life form higher than more primitive reptiles, such as the crocodilians, could be made to grow that fast and survive. Some of the replicators did, indeed, branch out into sidelines of producing larger reptiles and certain amphibians and huge eels for their hides and meat, but mostly for the income that could be plowed into the horrendously expensive replication projects.

"Then there was that *Tätzelwurm* thing, too; Bedford's not even mentioned it yet in these journals, but I recall it was a pure wonder for some time. For numberless generations, the peoples living in the Alps, the Pyrenees, the Carpathians, the Caucasus, the Urals and in various parts of Sweden, Norway, Finland and Iceland had been telling of these serpentine creatures, rarely seen. The scientific establishment had decided, early on, that the tales were rubbish, nothing but folk myths perpetuated with the purposes of gulling the gullible and frightening naughty children, and so had dismissed them.

"And, lo and behold, an Austro-Italian group of scientists, who happened to be in the Italian Alps for an entirely different reason, chanced to capture one of the things alive . . . and very, very pregnant! Careful examination in Torino proved that for all her snakelike appearance, the thing was an amphibian, predatory and exceedingly strong, vicious and, with her double rows of sharp, pointed teeth, exceedingly dangerous when aroused or cornered, though generally retiring by nature.

"The captive laid her eggs soon after capture. They were all taken out of the pool in her enclosure and transferred to tanks in which they were allowed to hatch. Almost immediately, someone got the idea of accelerating the maturations of some of the young, and so by the late nineties, almost every zoo of any size, worldwide, had a couple or more specimens of this distinctly unprepossessing creature, until so very recently considered but a figment of the fevered imaginations of ignorant, unlettered mountain peasants.

"I saw a few of them in various zoos, and they did nothing to thrill me. They were sort of a dirty brownish white, looking slick because of the mucus their smooth skins produced. Their front legs didn't exist and their rear ones were just little atrophied stumps. They really looked like big, thick earthworms—six or seven feet long and about as thick as my calf, I'd say—and annulated like earthworms, too; that is, they looked like earthworms until they opened their mouths. Hell, their heads were all toothy jaws.

"Their eyes were tiny and very thickly covered with skin; you couldn't see them if they weren't open, in fact. They preferred, lived most of their lives, in near-total darkness—in caves, deep fissures, peat bogs, under piles of rotting vegetation, only usually coming into the open at night. Apparently, it was finally decided after years of study of captive specimens, the pregnant female that had first been captured had been out by day only because she was making haste to a pool wherein to lay her eggs.

"The things ate anything animal that they could lay tooth to. They'd eat insects, worms, fish, other amphibians—including each other—reptiles, birds, mammals of any sort, eggs, dung of any provenance. Nor did their meat have to be fresh; they seemed to really prefer, to seek out, carrion. They consumed everything except bone—they lacked the proper dentition for that kind of diet, though if they happened to gulp down smaller bones or pieces of them, they seemed to have no trouble digesting them.

"The reason for the extraordinary flexibility of their bodies was revealed when there were enough specimens around to allow for killing and dissecting some of the creatures. Then it was found that save for the head, jaws and teeth and parts of the spine, the skeletons of the adults were virtually pliable cartilage, like the skeleton of the shark.

"Of course, experiments continued, but the last I heard

on the subject, no use—aside from display as curiosities—was ever found for them, except that their proven existence vindicated numberless generations of mountain people of numerous races and nationalities and indicted numberless generations of self-proclaimed scientists for the elitist snobs they had proved themselves to be, utterly lacking in imagination or curiosity, hidebound ultraconformists to their dying days.

"I wonder if that cat back there in the den area and those three cubs are, could be, descendants of this project that Bedford's group was to undertake? I've never seen any living feline with a set of upper cuspids as long as hers, and though none of the cubs seem to share that trait, it might be something that comes with adult teeth and is always absent in the milk teeth they now bear.

"He was writing about acquiring snow leopards, and her coat does look more than a bit like a snow leopard's—the few of the rare ones I saw in the flesh, a few skins I saw and pictures of them—but she's way too big to be any snow leopard. Even in her state of malnourishment and illness, she must weigh in at well over two hundred pounds, so how much more would a male of her breed weigh, I wonder?

"Speaking of which, if we do get her and the cubs back to the clans and they do work out in partnership with humans of our kind as well as I hope and pray that they do, we—meaning, originally, me—are going to have to try to seek out others of her type, and she avers that there are others hereabouts, though just where or how close she doesn't know. Even a solitary cat that size would require a pretty sizable chunk of territory to adequately feed itself, and if the breed are gregarious, even in pairs, you can more than double the territory involved, especially when they have litters in the process of weaning.

"Not only can I and the other men here communicate telepathically with the cat and her cubs, but she and to a lesser extent they seem really intelligent, reasoning creatures. Now, the big big question is: is her particular strain the only one that has this gift that can be so priceless to us—the clans—or do the other cats of her breed share in it?

"But, okay, say we can't find any of her kind, what do we do? We could inbreed it, breed the male cub back into her and into his two female siblings, of course. But there're always certain dangers in breeding and rebreeding an animal that closely and just keeping it up. So what choices do we have, huh? Just let this rare and wonderful strain die out? No, I can't countenance that alternative; cats like her and them could mean far too much to us—to the long-run survival of us all, clans and people. So, then, what can I do to perpetuate her and her promise?

"Find a big puma tom and try to take him alive and bring him back to top her? No, even if we could do it, I don't think it would work; those two breeds are just too vastly divergent. The puma, for all its size, is still considered to be *Felis*, same genus as all the small cats, while the furry lady in there is clearly some species of *Panthera*— tiger, lion, leopard and so on.

"So where do we find a member of the *Panthera* in the Rocky Mountains of North America? Of course, the only one that was native within the ten thousand or so years prior to the end of the last civilization was the jaguar, the cat the Mexicans call *tigre*, but I've never seen one of them this far north, though if they can live in the Andes as they do, I see no reason why such mountains as these

would daunt them. But could it be . . . ? Could it be that
the existence of this rare, long-toothed breed of cats living
and hunting these mountains is the reason that the jaguars
spreading slowly north from Old Mexico have never carved
themselves out a niche hereabouts? There's that to consider, too, and in further support of the theory, we've seen
damned little trace hereabouts of anything approaching the
size of a puma or a lynx, either, just a scat and a few
pawprints of one solitary bobcat, and not an awfully big
one at that.

"It's a long, hard journey down far enough south to be
certain of finding a jaguar or three, and if we go that far,
hell, we might as well cross over into California and see
about roping us a real leopard. Last time I was in Southern
California, there were both leopards and cheetahs to be
found there, even some tigers and a whole hell of a lot of
lions. They were why we had to leave, the good graze and
hunting notwithstanding—there were just too damned many
predators roaming about our herds and camps for comfort.

"And we're back to little Arabella Lindsay again, by
gum. It was her, constantly prodding at me orally and
telepathically, who was primarily responsible for my sug-
gestion to the chiefs that we find a pass, cross the ranges
and winter that year in Southern California. She was so
anxious to see with her own two eyes the cities I'd allowed
her to see in my memories.

"And she discovered to her sorrow that my memories
are the only place in which anyone will ever again see
them. According to reports at the time, I believe that the
vast Los Angeles area was struck by at least three and
perhaps as many as five missiles, so it's bound to still be
hot, radioactively speaking, and consequently I wouldn't
allow any of my people really close to it, but what I saw of

it from the hills to the west was truly heartbreaking when compared to my memories of better times.

"The missiles of course did very little real damage to most of the structures—what did them in was the horrific conflagrations that raged unchecked for as long as there was anything on which flames could feed. Also, it appeared that at some time between the time I left California and the time I returned with Arabella and the clans, there had been one or more really bad earthquakes in the Los Angeles area, and these had toppled anything standing after the effects of fires and years of natural decay. By then, there was precious little left to show above the abundant vegetation, the river and the numerous little lakes and tiny streams that man had ever settled or built there. That no one had resettled any part of the vast territory I ascribe to fear of radioactivity, no doubt passed on by word of mouth to each new generation of survivors, though a tribe of Mexican nomads we ran into farther south said that their forebears had tried to winter in the areas of rich graze and hunting on two occasions and had each time been forced to leave because of the hordes of large and small predators.

"So it just wouldn't do to take the clans and the herds back into California—well, not far into it, anyway. We'd have to find a relatively secure place with plenty of graze and water and enough game to feed us, then send a strong party down westward to find and rope a big, healthy male leopard, truss him up and bring him back. And that is a task that I don't look forward to, either, thank you kindly. We'll have to time it for when our furry lady is in or near her estrus, or we'll have to construct a cage to keep our leopard in until she is naturally receptive and fertile. And even then that mating may not take.

"No, I think the best thing for the clans to do is to bend their every effort toward finding more of her breed, around here, first, then farther afield if necessary, in other areas like this one."

His thoughts and schemes and fledgling plans were interrupted by an insistent scratching at the outer face of the door, and he leaned over and opened it to admit the largest of the three cubs. The beastlet stalked in, seated himself, wrapped his thick tail around his big paws and mindspoke his imperious demands.

"Killer-of-Two-Legs is hungry. He wants more of the thin milk that the two-legs make from white sand and water. Get it for him, *now*!"

"If it's milk you want," beamed Milo, "I suggest you take up the matter with your mother, for you and she and your sisters have drunk up all of the powdered milk that we found here."

"The Mother drives us away when we try to nurse," was the cub's reply. "Then get this cat some meat, a big, big piece. Get it *now*! Get it before Killer-of-Two-Legs hurts you."

"Here we go again," thought Milo to himself, slipping his hands back into his leather riding gloves with the thick cuffs of skirting-weight that reached almost to his elbows.

"Then go upstairs and tell one of those two-legs to hack you off a piece of the last kill and—"

"No!" The cub rippled a snarl that was amazingly deep to issue from so small a body. "Be warned, Two-Legs, this cat wants *fresh* meat, fresh, still warm and dripping blood, none of that old, cold meat, all icy and watery. You and the other two-legs go out and get meat for this cat, *now*! You will not be warned again."

"Do you hear the wind howling, little cat?" beamed

Milo. "A blizzard is raging outside this place, and no one can go out to hunt until it ends, until it's howled itself out, so you may have your choice: a chunk of frozen venison, a frozen elk steak or nothing at all. And I issue *you* warning: try attacking me again and I'll do to you just what I've done before; you'll hurt, not me."

But the warning did no slightest good, for without pause, the cub launched his furry body upward at Milo's face, his teeth bared, forelegs and paws spread, claws out, pure murder in his eyes.

Milo's powerful backhand slap took the cub in the sensitive nose with enough force to not only negate all the power of his spring but to actually reverse it and send the twenty-odd pounds of fur and flesh, muscle and bone tumbling back to finally thud against a concrete wall and sprawl in a corner of the small room, barely conscious, his big head having struck the wall first and hardest.

Milo sought out the mother cat's mind and beamed, "My lady, I once more have had to hurt the male cub."

"You are good," she beamed back. "Had he not deserved to be hurt, you would not have hurt him any more than this one would have hurt him. I hunger. So do the cubs. You two-legs will bring us meat soon?"

"Yes, it will be soon, my lady," Milo silently replied, then, still keeping a wary eye on his furry antagonist, now beginning to tremble all over and whimper in the corner, he beamed upstairs to the first mind he could range, Djim Linsee. "Djim, the cat and the cubs are hungry, so one of you go up atop that tower and see if you can hack enough meat off one of those carcasses for the four of them. There should still be enough to go around, even if this blizzard lasts for another two days."

"It will be done, Uncle Milo," replied Djim, adding,

"Yes, there is still much meat frozen up there. We are making a stew here, with deer and elk and some of the things from the old times that you found down there. It will be good, Uncle Milo, it already smells good, very, very good it smells."

"I'll just bet it does, Djim," beamed Milo, grinning. "But you and the others take it easy on those powders and dried herbs. Not all of them mix together well, flavoringwise, and when those are gone, there'll be no more . . . ever. The finding of these was the wildest chance find out of inconceivable odds against such a cache surviving this long intact and still being accessible. Besides, too much of or a wrong mixture of some of those spices eaten by people not accustomed to them can make you violently ill, make you so sick you'll pray for death. So beware."

Memory of the first time the naive nomads had experimented on their own with the hoard of spices and condiments from Bedford's store of foodstuffs and flavorings still could bring a smile to his lips. Some one of them had elected to dump a full three-ounce jar of piquinita peppers, most of a jar of hot curry powder, some cracked peppercorns, powdered ginger root, whole cloves and some ounces of tabasco into an otherwise innocent stew of venison and freeze-dried vegetables. The result had been a dish hot enough to have seared out any Mexican, Korean, Thai or Hunan palate, and but a single mouthful of the stuff had been enough to send the nomads racing up the steel stairs to the top of the tower, there to jump down to where they could cram handfuls of snow into their burning mouths without pause or conscious thought until their sufferings had begun to ease. Milo had finally speared the larger chunks of meat from out the pot, scooped up as many of the vegetables as he could, dumped and rinsed and scoured the pot, then filled it with clear water, added fresh fuel to the fire and boiled the retrieved food long enough to make it at least palatable, if tough and very much overcooked. The much shocked and thoroughly abashed nomads had been very wary of the strange bottles and jars for a while and were but just beginning to hesitantly try some of them once more in their cooking.

To the gasping, whimpering cub, Milo beamed, "I suggest that you go back to the den with your mother and sisters now. Other two-legs will presently be bringing down meat for you all."

"You *hurt* this cat!" was the cub's reply. "*You* hurt Killer-of-Two Legs . . . and he will not soon forget it."

"Good," he beamed. "Remember that hurting well, and whenever you think of attacking me or one of the others again, recall that the sure outcome will be more hurting of you."

"You remember, Two-Legs," beamed the cub bitterly. "You are bigger and stronger, now, but Killer-of-Two-Legs will be bigger than you, one day. On that day, he will claw loose your belly-parts, he will rip out your throat and drink your hot blood, he will—"

Milo broke in with his own beaming. "He will be dead before he so much as touches claw or tooth to any one of us two-legs, rather. Enter your mother's memories and learn from them just how difficult it is to slay two-legs. Learn how easily I slew, in her sight and hearing, a dozen or more adult wolves on the day I came first into the den. You must quickly learn and accept a fact that your mother and your sisters already have learned and accepted: you cats and we two-legs are not enemies, but now friends; we are, however, not in any way servants, one of the other, but partners against the rest of this hard, cruel world and its adversities. One of us does not order the other or feel any compunction to do so, for we both willingly work together for the common good, as true Kindred should. In this and in no other way can cat and two-legs forge out a secure bond between us.''

Chapter VII

Project *feethami* had wound up with not two but three of the nearly extinct snow leopards, two females and one male; all three of these cats were zoo-born and -bred, and the largest weighed only some forty-six or so kilos; this was the male, and the females ran only a bit over two-thirds of that weight. The white jaguar which finally arrived, on the other hand, was quite another matter; he had been trapped while roaming wild as a full-grown adult, and a couple of years of caged captivity had not done much either to improve his temper or to reduce his desire to regain his freedom. Nor was he at all small, being twice as heavy as the male snow leopard, his weight spread over a longer-legged, rangier frame. He had cost over twice what the total had been for all three of the snow leopards, and so Bedford prayed that he would prove to be worth so large a chunk of the project's already slim budget.

There were two other cats, both females. In order to obtain the initial pair of snow leopards, Bedford had had no option but to buy the two ringers—which the dealer had apparently been unable to unload on anyone else—which were derived of a bankruptcy sale that had marked the

end of some underfunded European project. He was not
sure just what to call them. The dealer had claimed that
they were spotted lions, and they did bear a fleeting resem-
blance to leonine shape, but they were neither of them any
larger than the white jaguar, lacked both the bony spur and
characteristic tuft on the end of the tail and had upper
cuspids as long in proportion to their heads and jaws as
snow leopards. Although they were about two years old—to
judge from their overall physical and sexual development—
their reddish-tawny coats were speckled thickly on the
back and sides with darker spots, with a few more lighter
and less distinct ones even extending down the legs and
onto the tail. Whatever they were, they were gentle, obviously used to the presence of humans and cooperative.

Bedford had, on the journey back with the four cats
which would join the one female snow leopard already
arrived, been very worried about the reception of the two
strange felines. But he found he need not have so fretted,
for Singh, Stekowski, Ruth Marberg and Zepur Baronian
had all been ecstatic over the chance acquisition.

In the staff meeting later on the day he and the four cats
had arrived back, Singh had explained their exceeding joy
to him. "James, you are of course familiar with the recent
success and the patenting of the *Panthera spelaea* replications by the Greek-Yugoslavian group? Well, what you
may not know is that their efforts, though eminently successful, of course, were not truly original. No, there was a
somewhat earlier project aimed at the selfsame replication:
Panthera spelaea.

"That project was backed by an Italian investment group,
and it overreached itself along many financial fronts. When
there was no more money, almost all of the project's
physical assets and records were brought up by the hur-

riedly formed Greek-Yugoslavian group; they even hired on some of the original group's personnel. All of this took place about eighteen months ago, and just how, at that time, two little cubs of no more than four or six months of age went astray and into the hands of this animal dealer, I cannot at all begin to imagine. If only he had known, he could have set almost any price for them and received it, too, had it gladly paid to him by the then-ongoing project in the Balkans.

"Awaiting only more detailed examination, we all here are firmly convinced that those two specimens are, can be nothing but, replications or reproduced examples of the *Panthera spelaea*—a spotted lion, somewhat smaller than the average of our extant lions, generally adapted to colder weather, denning in caves and possibly originally a predator of montane forests, like the uncia or snow leopard of today and, most likely, the extinct *Panthera feethami*, as well."

"The unexpected possession of these two cats should be a really tremendous advantage to us, to our own project, Jim," said Dr. Baronian. "We already have the *feethami* material in the lab freezer, so whenever the jaguar gets here, we can start to work. With all of us together—"

"But it will not be all of us together, Dr. Baronian!" snarled Harel, who had been sitting in glum silence since the beginning of the meeting. "I told you all from the very outset, I will never have anything to do with, take any tiniest part in, replicating any damned, blood-drinking, murderous predator species.

"What now is to become of the bovines out there? Are they all to just be left to starve in the snow? Or is it the predaceous Mr. Bedford's intention to have them slaughtered and butchered, one by one, to feed those stinking, treacherous cats . . . and his own unnatural meat-eating tendencies?'' For the first time in several days, the big, beefy man emphasized his question by slamming his broad palm down on the table before him, sullen hatred in the stare he glared at the group at the other end of the table.

Bedford sighed resignedly. ''Look, Dr. Harel, I'll go through it one more time. See if you can get it into your head this time around. While I did order the skinning and butchering and hanging of the carcass of that wisent cow, I did not order her killed and I had nothing to do with the killing of her; she was killed in order to save Dr. Stekowski's life. Yes, I ate and continue to eat of the carcass, just as I eat of the other meats in that cooler out there. I like game, this is excellent game-hunting country hereabouts, I hunt and so too do some other members of our staff, so there will continue to be game aging in the cooler no matter how much that fact displeases you.

''Insofar as feeding the cats is concerned, I've obtained some special licenses from the State Game Department to take elk and deer year-round from certain areas, and should the hunting fail at any time, I'll have sides of beef brought up here for them, or mutton or goat or horse or whatever. Your precious shaggy bison and cattle and bastard cross-breeds will not be bothered, please believe me, whether or not you happen to be around to watch over them.''

Harel's bushy eyebrows elevated markedly. ''And just why, Mr. Bedford, would I not be here to watch over the bovines, eh? Have you conspirators schemed to rid your-selves of me, then? To try to buy my departure, perhaps? Disabuse yourselves; my contract reads 'until successful completion of ongoing project or severance upon payment of mutually agreed-upon sum.' In order to buy my departure, you will have to pay me four million dollars, in cash, please.''

''*Lieber Gott!*'' commented Dr. Marberg. ''No one could ever accuse you of undervaluing yourself, Doctor. That sum represents two-thirds of the amount we now have for the entire year, unless we can replicate in less time than that. You know that, too, don't you? You would depart happily only if you could know that you had done your best to sink this project before it was hardly begun. You are truly scum, aren't you, Harel? If you cannot have everything your own selfish, peculiar way, you'd willingly, gladly spoil it for everyone else.''

''*Saure Ziege!*'' sneered Harel. ''No matter what fables this Jim of yours has spun, I happen to know the truth of the matter. When his grandfather died, he left an estate of over five hundreds of millions of dollars, so there is far more money available than this pig of a James Bedford would have you and me think. He just wants to get everything cheap, like all capitalist pigs since the very beginning of time. You may all come just that cheaply, but I don't.''

Bedford shook his head slowly and said, with exasperation in his voice, ''You babbling fool, Harel, you think you know far more than you actually do in this matter. Yes, my grandfather's estate was sizable, even after the whopping taxes on it were duly paid in full. But you seem to think I inherited all of it. Nothing could be farther from the truth, in actuality; my total—total, Harel, all—inheritance was a bit over forty-one million dollars, but not in the form of cash, rather in investments which pay out to me an income of not quite five million dollars per calendar year, out of which I have to pay taxes. Almost my entire yearly stipend has gone directly into your lackluster, long-drawn-out Project *latifrons* during the last few years, for the little that you appreciated that fact. What little of a bank account the project has left as of right now is what little is left of this year's stipend.

"So far as the principal is concerned, you silly ass, I could be starving and in rags and I still could not touch one red cent of it. Don't you know anything about inheritance?

"I had been intending to pay you enough to relocate, along with my personal note for a bit more in time. I also found a slot for you, one with a project that I think you'll like, one in which your experience with island fauna will be valuable. Dr. Fleming Van Natta and a group sponsored by the State of California and in part funded by the Steakley Foundation will shortly commence a project to replicate the so-called dwarf mammoths on those same Channel Islands whereon the fossils of them have been found. I spoke with Dr. Van Natta, told him of you and of your work on Cyprus, and he seems quite anxious to meet with you, to have you as a member of his group."

"Jim, that was such a nice thing to do for Dr. Harel." said Dr. Marberg. "You are basically a nice, sweet man, you—"

"He is a meddling fool!" snarled Harel, red-faced. "I have no intention of leaving this project for another until either we achieve a patentable replication of *Bison latifrons* or I am paid my four millions of dollars. Do I make clear myself?

"Now, you will immediately reconnect the videophone, Bedford. I must have conversation with Dr. Ivanov."

"Relative to what, Harel?" demanded Bedford shortly.

"I do not at all enjoy to be questioned, Bedford," replied Harel frigidly. "But I nonetheless will tell you of this. I must have another . . . no, two more wisent cows delivered to this location as soon as possible. Also, he spoke when last I rang him up of some *Bos gaurus hubbacki* which have been bred up from stock obtained in Malaysia and acclimated to Siberia. I want at least a pair of them.''

"My God!" Bedford smote his forehead forcefully with the heel of one hand. To the others he said, "Have you understood all that I've been saying here today? Or did I unconsciously slip into Pushtu, Algonquin or Basque? I don't think he's understood a single word I've said.

"Dr. Harel, Project *latifrons* is on indefinite hold, can you comprehend that fact? There will be no more funds expended on the acquisition of new or replacement stock for it. Indeed, there will be no funds at all spent on it other than what is absolutely necessary to keep the existing herd alive . . . and that only until and if we can find good placements for them elsewhere, with zoos or another project."

"No, Bedford, it is you who have not understood," stated Harel grimly. "The mere possession of those stinking, bloodthirsty cats does not mean that Project *latifrons* is to end. To end the project must be voted upon by the whole of the staff, and I say no. How say you, Dr. Stekowski?" he demanded in a peculiar, ominous tone, his hard eyed gaze fixed upon the old man.

Stekowski's lips moved, but no sound emerged. He tried again and said, in a half-whisper, "No, no, Dr. Harel."

Harel smiled smugly and had started to speak when Stekowski spoke again. "No, Dr. Harel, I do not agree with you. Not this time, not ever again. I do not truly know just why you felt that we all must be sent off into the *latifrons* business, which you must have realized would require far more time than we could find the funding to support, but I can guess why.

"The manner in which you forced my acquiescence to your schemes for so long was despicable, there is no other term to describe it. It was quite effective, naturally, as you must have well known that it would be. But the good God in whom you do not believe has loosed your hateful hold on me, He has taken my dear brother to His bosom, he can never again be hurt by those I think you serve, Dr. Harel."

For the first time he could recall, Bedford saw Harel look stunned, not a little perturbed and clearly worried. "What of you, Dr. Singh?" he asked, licking his lips several times, as if they had become suddenly very dry.

The East Indian shrugged. "If we had had more time and money, then the *latifrons* affair might have been a complete success and gained us a patent . . . though I doubt there would've, could've been much of a market for the replications after that. But as matters now stand, with the excellent prospects that we have been so fortuitously granted in Mr. Bedford's newest acquisitions, I think that Project *feethami* will quickly result in both a patent and a ready, enthusiastic and probably large market. Therefore, I say that we formally end Project *latifrons* and formally commence our Project *feethami* as of this date."

"You Hindu cretin!" Harel half shouted from a near-livid face.

Before he could say more, Singh bristled with the closest thing to anger Bedford had ever seen him display. "As you well should know after our close association over these last years, Dr. Harel, I am no Hindu, I am rather a Sikh."

"Pah!" snorted Harel. "One of you swine is alike to all the rest. Need I ask how you say, Dr. Marberg?"

"I say yes, Dr. Harel. Let us begin Project *feethami*. It was to have been our original project, and you have seen it delayed for quite long enough," she answered calmly.

"Unrepentant fascist!" he hissed, enraged. "Nazi bitch!"

She shook her head, displaying no anger, only disgust. "Your research has been incomplete, Dr. Harel, in this instance. Some of my father's relatives were Nazis, yes, but he was not. No, he emigrated from Germany to the United States with my mother . . . who was Jewish."

"Your husband was a Nazi, I know that much!" shouted Harel, beating the side of a fist on the table.

"Klaus Marberg was a member of the Hitler Jugend, Dr. Harel," she answered. "It was then a totalitarian government in Germany, and he never had a choice. But although he regretted even that slight association with Nazism until his dying day, since he was only eleven years of age in 1945, when the war and Nazism both ended, he could not have contributed much to Nazism, the war or any atrocities. . . . Dr. Harel, what does any of this baseless slander of me, my father and my late husband have to do with the matter at hand here, under discussion? I can discern no slightest degree of relevance, the one matter to the other."

"Oh, shut up, you withered old crone!" snapped Harel. Then, "Well, Dr. Baronian, Armenian scientist, do you stand with me?"

Her lips curled. "Yes, I'm a scientist, and yes, I am of Armenian heritage, but I am first and foremost an American, and I spit on you and your asinine *latifrons* project, Dr. Harel. And I am sick unto death of your beans and greens and tasteless, ill-seasoned messes of boiled grains. I want meat!"

He glowered at her and opened his lips to speak, but she

spoke again first. "No more veiled threats, Dr. Harel,
don't waste your breath. Yes, I do have a scattering of
very distant relatives still living in the Soviet Armenia and
in Syria, but they've lived there all their lives and so I
seriously doubt that what I do or do not do here, on this
project, could in any way seriously affect them; I've thought
it all out while I lay in my bed of nights trying to digest
those godawful vegetarian meals of yours. Christ, I've
never before in all my life experienced such horrible gas
pains, eating as you do, it's no longer any wonder to me
why you're always so nasty to those around you."

Bedford nodded. "I say yes, too. So it's settled, Dr.
Harel: Project *latifrons* is hereby canceled and Project
feethami is begun. If you want to and will work on the
new project, I'm certain that you could contribute—"

"*NO!*" Harel, now utterly livid, sprang suddenly to his
feet, so forcefully shoving back his chair that it slammed
onto its back and then slid on to crash into the baseboard.
"*No*, I refuse to be bound by this outrageous, fascistic,
capitalist conspiracy against me! I will institute lawsuit. I
tell you, you cannot so easily misuse me, so flagrantly to
disregard my wishes, so insubordinately to disobey my
orders. When I am done you all will wish that never had
you allowed this spawn of foul exploiters of workers and
the peasants to lead you from the right and proper and
bring those accursed, filthy cats to this place."

"What?" remarked Bedford, a note of mockery clear in
his tone. "No threats of physical violence against us this
time, Harel? No more fist-shakings and table-poundings
and wall-beatings? No real tantrum at all? Why is this,
pray tell? Did your masters warn you against any more
exercises of such behavior . . . or did my fist in your solar
plexus painfully point out to you that you can only brow-

beat and intimidate those who cannot or will not return blow for attempted blow? For all your size and strength, your bluster and violent posturings, you're just a bully and a coward, after all, aren't you, *tovarisch*?''

With a wordless roar, Harel grasped his blackthorn stick and stalked down the length of the table, using his free hand to sweep Singh brutally hard into the wall, swinging a cane-cut at Zepur Baronian but, thanks to her quick reflexes, missing her. His eyes were bloodshot and blazing, bulging from their sockets in the intensity of his rage, and he again was grasping the stick as if it were an edged straight-sword, his right hand a couple of inches above shoulder level, the length of the stick back almost parallel to the floor.

As he drew near, he hissed, ''A coward, Bedford? To show you who the coward is I will. To whimper and scream and cry piteously for mercy and surcease you will before done with you I am. To see much of your blood and your tears, I mean and—''

Bedford arose slowly, almost languidly. ''I'd hoped you'd feel that way, Comrade Harel. I came prepared to this meeting today, you see—that's why I deliberately provoked you.''

Reaching beneath the table, he took from where it leaned against a table leg a dark-stained, brass-handled rattan cane of antique appearance, almost as long as Harel's blackthorn stick, though a bit more slender.

Placing himself directly in the bigger man's line of advance, he assumed a fencer's stance—feet heel to heel and at right angles one to the other, the right toe pointed at his opponent, the left knee flexed, only his right side presented, the rattan cane held easily at guard in the fourth, its brassbound tip winking upward in the direction of Harel's throat. With two long steps, the big man closed the distance and swung the blackthorn down at the smaller man's bare head. Singh gasped, Stekowski's lips moved soundlessly, Dr. Baronian moaned and shut her eyes, hunching her body, awaiting the fearsome sound of the hardwood striking flesh and bone, but Ruth Marberg just sat in silence, watching the unfolding of the combat carefully, the ghost of a smile haunting her lips.

Gracefully, James Bedford swayed his body and head from out the path of the long stick, his feet never moving, his legs but barely, even when the side of the stick brushed against them. Then, at the split second the tip of the stick smote the hard floor, his left hand took a grip on Harel's wrist while he backed sufficiently to give himself room enough to deliver a vicious cut with the rattan to the side of Harel's head, the rattan punishing flabby jowl, ear and upper neck, alike.

Crying out in surprise, shock and pain, Harel stepped back reflexively, jerking out of Bedford's grasp. Also reflexively, he put his hand to his left jowls and ear, then stared stupidly for a moment at the bright-red bloodsmear on his palm. With a bestial growl, his big teeth bared in fury, he took a two-hand swing at the composed, hated face before him.

Bedford ducked easily beneath that swing and the stick struck the wall, the shock of the impact clearly to be seen in every inch of Harel's big, paunchy body, and before he could so much as think of recovery, Bedford had split his right ear as well, and had himself recovered and was once again in his fencing stance, his guard now in the seventh, pointing vaguely in the direction of Harel's feet.

Drs. Singh and Baronian had retreated to join Drs. Stekowski and Marberg on the other side of the table. Stekowski still was shaking his old head and moving his lips, but Ruth Marberg's ghost of a smile had fleshed out to a real, tooth-flashing grin.

"You, too, should have learned how to fence, Dr. Harel," she chided the big, shaken, puffing, bleeding man. "In your clumsy hands, a stick is only a mere club with which to beat helpless, unarmed victims. Jimmy will show you how a proper gentleman can use a cane, won't you, Jimmy? Do they no longer teach the light sword in the USSR, then?"

"You wrong me, Doctor." He huffed a near-growl. "You slander me; I am an Israeli, you know that."

"Yes." She nodded brusquely, her smile flown away. "So you and your records say . . . but men, like records, have been known to lie. *Nicht wahr*?"

"Have you had enough, Dr. Harel?" inquired Bedford, conversationally. "You throw your stick over the table and mine will follow it, but you throw yours first. I don't trust you."

"Yes, please, please stop, I beg of you both," Dr. Stekowski pled, tears glittering in his eyes. "Remember, violence is the last refuge of the incompetent."

"You say so?" asked Bedford, then added in a scathing tone, "Then that eminent self-proclaimed Israeli scientist Dr. Harel, here, must own unquestioned some kind of all-time world-class record for incompetence. Wouldn't you think so, Ruth?"

Too winded, still, to really growl, much less roar, the battered bully took a fresh, crushing grip on his now-scarred blackthorn stick; all could see his muscles tensing for another attack.

But suddenly, the tip of the rattan swept forward, feinting at the bigger man's eyes, and as both stick and free left hand rose to defend, the deceitful rattan dropped down, was drawn back just far enough to allow for a hard, short thrust to Harel's bulging midriff. It struck between two of the straining shirt buttons, seeming to sink inches deep in the flabby flesh before striking denser tissue.

The afflicted man broke wind resoundingly, his eyes looked fit to burst from out of their sockets, and a gasping whine was the best that he could mouth. His left hand descended to grab the rattan cane, but its grip was so weak and fitful that Bedford had but a fleeting moment of resistance when he withdrew his weapon, which he then used to deliver a shrewd, powerful blow to the big man's right wrist; when Harel still did not drop the blackthorn stick, Bedford grimaced, again raised his cane and slammed it down, this time across the back of Harel's right hand. The big man screamed and his hand relaxed to let the blackthorn stick thump onto the floor at his feet.

Whining, taking his right hand gingerly into his left, he tried to move his fingers, half screamed again and looked up at Bedford, tears cascading down his chubby cheeks, a near-sob in his voice. "Damn you, you brutal bastard! My hand, my hand, you have broken it! Broken at least one of my metacarpals, you have, all four of them, perhaps."

"And what did you intend to do to me, Harel?" asked Bedford, blandly. "It seems to me that I recall threats to the effect of seeing blood and tears, of hearing whimpers, screams and sobs. Well, you should now feel happy, fulfilled, for you've now seen blood and if you looked in a mirror just now you'd see tears, too . . . but both of these substances your own, of course, not mine. As for sound effects, you've screamed and sobbed, so far. So tell me, please, just what would I have to do further to you to draw one good, audible whimper out of you? Would another blow on the back of your right hand do it? Hold it out here and we'll see—we don't want you disappointed, after all.''

When Bedford made as if to raise his cane, Harel hugged his swelling, reddening hand to his body and stumbled back, shaking his head so forcefully that tears from his cheeks and blood from his two split ears flew out in all directions. "No, no, please! No, of you I beg, Mr. Bedford, sir. Please to not hurt me any more, please. To leave I will, *I promise*. I promise, never again to hear of me will any of you. If to the Van Natta project you wish me to go, then there I will go, tomorrow, tonight, I swear it. But do not to hit my hand again, please . . . please?''

Surrendering his consciousness momentarily to an atavistic urge to sadistically toy with, mercilessly taunt an injured and helpless prey, Bedford brought his rattan cane up to guard in sixth and smoothly, with obvious deliberation, slid his right foot forward, toward Harel, bringing his left foot back up in place against the right.

"Come, come, Dr. Harel," he said coldly, "you've given us pleas, now, but still no whimpers. Can we not all hear just one little whimper?''

He started when he felt a hand on his left shoulder, started and almost struck out again at the cowering, injured man.

"Jimmy," said Ruth Marbert's low, controlled voice, "this you now are doing is like him, not like the Jimmy I know and care for. This is just as a . . . a something like Dr. Harel would behave, not as would a man, a man like you. Stop torturing him. He is now hurt and hurting and without spirit to fight. You and your cane broke more of him than just his bones. So let him be, I beg you, just let him be. I'll attend to his injuries now.''

Slowly, Bedford relaxed, allowed the cane to sink from the guard position. He suddenly felt utterly exhausted, almost limp. Harel's tear-swimming eyes watched the terrible cane's slow descent with bated breath. When Singh and Zepur, having come from behind him, around the far end of the table, pushed a chair to the backs of his knees and helped him to settle in it, the big, battered man sank his head upon his chest and began to sob, raggedly, whimpering like a whipped child.

"Jim," said Dr. Marberg, "you and Dr. Singh will have to help him down the hall to my lab. I need to find out just how badly he's hurt. If those bones in his hand are indeed broken, then we'll have to call a copter to fly him down to a clinic or a hospital. I'm a fair general sawbones as well as being a medical researcher, but orthopedics was never my specialty.''

Having with great surprise and by supporting most of his weight with the cane and the table edge made it up to his chair, Bedford shook his head. "No, Ruth, not quite yet. There're still some things we have to get straight, here and now. Get Harel some aspirin and a cup of coffee. Hell, I could use a cup, too.''

When all again were in their usual places, Jim Bedford took a folder from his case and unloosed its tiestring, then took out some typewritten sheets.

"Dr. Stekowski," he began, "I want both you and Dr. Baronian to tell us all just how Dr. Harel was threatening you to ensure your cooperation with his dictates and will on this project. After you have done so, I'll tell you all some things that you likely do not know about Dr. Harel. Well, Dr. Stekowski?''

Stekowski sighed. "Mr. Bedford, when my wife and I defected, many years ago, it made for a hard choice for me, at least. She had been orphaned during the Great Patriotic War against Germany, but I had to leave behind an elder brother and his wife. My sister-in-law died within a few years, of breast cancer. But when Dr. Harel first came to me, my brother still lived, a very old man, but still alive.

"Dr. Harel told me that he was going to join our staff, that I might retain the ostensible leadership and the title, but that I would do exactly as he ordered in all things. He showed me very recent three-dimensional stills of my brother at his home in Wroclaw, then told me all the terrible things that could befall the feeble old man were I to not become his man, were I not to redirect our project to bovid rather than felid animals.

"I loved my late brother, Mr. Bedford. He and his wife cared for me, virtually reared me, when our parents died. They saw to my education, licked boots and paid bribes to see to my higher studies. They in no way tried to discourage the defections of me and my wife, though they must surely have known that they would be made to suffer for those defections. Suffer they did, too. So I felt that I could not risk the possibility that a brutal and barbaric government would heap further sufferings upon my old, frail, ill brother; despite everything, I just could not risk it. Therefore, I became Dr. Harel's creature. I betrayed you all to him and to his nefarious schemes.

"However, within the last week, I have been in receipt of a letter from an old family friend. It told of the natural demise of my brother. He now is with God and beyond any sufferings that anyone could inflict upon him. He never had any children, for some reason, and I have no other relatives there of any degree of real closeness, so this monster here has lost his bestial hold upon me.

"I have caused you all much time and funding and distress, but in like circumstances, I must admit that I would behave in no other way, for ties of blood are close among us Slavs. I can in no way correct that which I have done and allowed to be done; therefore, I must tender my resignation from the group."

While Stekowski had been speaking, recounting in his low, slow, sad voice the cruel choice he had been forced to make, Ruth Marberg had begun to cry softly, but at his final words, she had dashed away her tears. "Oh, you dear, sweet, gentle, gallant, honorable old fool," she said, "you are the very heart and soul of our group, you *cannot* resign, for lacking you, there is no group, can be no project."

Bedford nodded, swallowing earnestly to clear the massive lump from out his throat. "Forget any thought of resignation, Dr. Stekowski, do you hear me? Why you did what you did can be easily understood by any compassionate person. Under like circumstances, faced with so bitter a choice, I'd like to think that I, too, would place loved ones first. Let us put hatred where hatred and disgust are clearly due: upon the filthy swine who did it to you, that thing down there." He waved in Harel's direction, then looked at his hand, and slowly wiped it on his coat.

"But . . . but, you don't understand, any of you," spluttered Harel. "You see, I too had no choice, they had threatened all of my family still living in Russia unless I—"

"*Shut up!*" snapped Bedford, adding, "Just save your desperate lies, Comrade Vladimir Markov. I had you investigated in great detail, investigated very thoroughly by a number of people and agencies in several countries, going back for years. Those investigators and I probably know about as much about you now as anyone living does, and presently I'll be reading the salient points of the full report for the edification of the group, and *then* you can spin your fables and lies. I've always enjoyed skeet and trap shooting, and I think I'll derive great pleasure in the shooting down of whatever misrepresentations you cast out before us.''

Chapter VIII

After so long a time that Milo had all but given him up for dead of cold or wolves or misfortune, Dik Esmith arrived below the plateau with five other Horseclansmen, a half-dozen packhorses and a small remuda of remounts. When once the newcomers and Milo's party had set up the yurt and set to constructing a protective corral for the horses against a spot at the base of the plateau, Milo squatted with Dik and a sub-chief of Clan Linsee, one Alex.

"How far behind you are the main party?" demanded Milo. "How many more days until they arrive, Dik?"

Dik remained silent, deferring to the Linsee sub-chief, but looked uncomfortable. It was Alex Linsee who replied.

"Uncle Milo, my brother and the other chiefs met in council on this matter and they decided that, all things considered, they dare not send out any more warriors than those with me here. But after the thaw commences, they will come up here, all four of the clans together. This clansman you sent back averred that game was to be easily found up here, but still the chiefs sent some packloads of hard cheese, dried herbs and roots, smoked fish and fat-paste for your party and for us, who will remain with you until after the thaw begins and the clans are come.''

"Now what's all this about four clans, Alex Linsee?" demanded Milo. "When my original hunting party left camp there were but the two—Linsee and Esmith. And just why do the chiefs feel that they dare not send out a larger party of warriors than your measly six? What has happened down there on the plain since I left?"

Both the sub-chief and Dik Esmith sighed. "It's a bitter hard winter, Uncle Milo," said Alex Linsee in preamble. "Game is scarce on the plains, and the wolfpacks run large and very fierce with their hunger. So dangerous are they in their numbers that not only folk and kine must be protected from them but even the largest and strongest of our hounds, are any to survive until the thaw.

"As if all that were not enough and more than enough, though, shortly after you and your hunters left, the very clan camp was attacked of a night by rovers not of Kindred ilk. Silently, they crept in upon us, silent as serpents in the snow, and only mere happenstance revealed them to one of the herd guards in time to save cattle and camp and clans. They were driven off with losses, in the end, but the fight was hard and long and costly to us, as well.

"As for Clans Makawlee and Baikuh, they were encamped miles to the southeast of us. Attacked as were we, but by vastly more numerous foemen, they broke camp and fled toward the higher country until their scouts chanced to meet a party of our hunters and decided to make common camp with us for mutual protection from these non-Kindred marauders. As the poor Makawlees and Baikuhs had lost all of their sheep and most of the goats and cattle and even some of their horses, no difficulties in combining camps was seen by my chief or the Esmith.''

"There were too many nomads to fight, then?" asked Milo.

Dik Esmith shook his head. "Oh. there has been fighting and killing . . . and dying, too, Uncle Milo. Immediately the stockade and brushwalls had been expanded, enlarged to hold the new folk and kine, my chief set the eldest and youngest and the matrons to guard it, then took out almost all the warriors and the maiden-archers. They found those who were pursuing the Makawlees and the Baikuhs, ambushed them and put to scattered flight those who survived the ensuing battle.

"Then some of the younger warriors and the maidens backtracked the non-Kindred to an ancient, ruined Dirtman town. They fired the wagon-tents and thatched roofs with arrows, ran off all the few animals there, slew some of the folk, but rode back without taking the time or risk to pillage.

"It was as well that they acted just so, for my chief and his victors arrived back at the clans' encampment to find it under heavy assault from another aggregation of non-Kindred rovers—those who had earlier tried that night attack, along in company with certain others of their unsavory ilk. With many of his own victors wounded already, he and they were hard pressed to even hold their own against so many, but the timely arrival of the party of maiden-archers saved the day for the right . . . but not quite in time to save the life of my chief." Dik's voice caught in his throat and he paused, his pale eyes swimming in unshed tears.

Milo reached across to grip the young man's arm hard, in wordless expression of sympathy and shared grief. "He was a good man, Dik. I will miss him. But he now rides the boundless plains of Wind. And, knowing him as I did, I am certain he went to Wind in great glory, glory which

"Speaking of which, Van," asked Bedford almost casually, "do you still hold those black belts?"

"Why, of course," responded the blond scientist. "Why?"

"Then," said Bedford, "Harel poses no danger to you . . . so long as you make certain he has no access to firearms and doesn't sneak up behind you. Sandy O'Malley will be in your group, too, won't she? Van, can you imagine what she would leave of that tub of lard if he tried to get rough with her?"

At this, Van Natta was moved to real, honest laughter. "And she looks so tiny, so helpless, so fragile, too. Remember when those punks tried to force her into an old car in the south parking lot that time, Jim?"

Grinning at the memory, Bedford replied, "And she rammed the head of the biggest one through a closed window? Yes, I remember it well. It could've gotten sticky, too, if John II hadn't said his few words on it—a few words was all the old man ever needed to say to clear up almost anything short of a full-fledged shooting war. The cops just could not bring themselves to believe that little Sandy had committed all the carnage they found on the scene.

"So, with two like you and Sandy around, I just can't see an unarmed Harel being any danger to you, out on your island, Van. So say you'll take him on and handle him in the way I'll outline and I'll tell you all I told John III. Okay?"

In Kyoto, Dr. Hara was really enthusiastic about the new project, especially so when he told her of his accidental buying of the two *Panthera spelaeus* replications. But, far more important to him and to the Project *feethami*, she agreed to present his request for funding to the board of the investors she advised on replication matters and seemed most confident of a sizable amount of forthcoming monies.

He boarded his plane for Washington, D.C., in much better spirits than when last he had left Japan. Despite the favorable reception and heartening words of the Japanese scientist, there was still the possibility that the investors would entertain reservations about investing any meaningful amounts in a project that was just now barely off the ground, a project that had been a failure in Canada and had been once delayed by his own group. Therefore, he felt it wise to shake every money tree within his reach.

When his Uncle Taylor saw the three-dimensional prints of the two spotted lions, the snow leopards and the white jaguar, he smiled broadly enough to reveal almost every tooth and nodded his head with its thick mane of snowy hair—both teeth and hair looking even whiter in contrast to his tanned face.

"Dammit, Jim, that's where you should've been headed all along, you know. I have high regard for our fine Israeli allies, always have, and my voting record bears me out, too; I'm certain that in a number of ways this Israeli scientist is a very smart, a brilliant man, but his act of steering all of you off on that damned bison business was stupid . . . but I suppose even the best of us make mistakes, it's part of being human."

James Bedford laughed. "I doubt you'll lose any Jewish-bloc votes over criticizing him, Uncle Taylor. He's an Israeli only because he was sent there, planted there deliberately by the Russians, you know. His real name is Dr. Vladimir Markov, he took his doctorate in Russia, only studied in Israel until he had managed to get himself invited to join the dwarf fauna project and then left that one suddenly and for no reason that any of them can understand to emigrate here and bull his way onto the Stekowski group's board.''

''James,'' said the senator quietly, ''I sincerely hope that you have access to substantial documented or documentable proof of these terrible slanders of this man, this immigrant scientist from one of our most faithful and loyal allied nations. Even here, within my private office, we are certainly being overheard by someone . . . likely, by a number of someones; privacy no longer exists here, not for anyone.''

Nodding, James Bedford took from his case a metal cylinder, set it before his uncle and scribbled rapidly on a scrap of the senator's heavy, embossed notepaper. ''*Full files here. Reports from U.S. & foreign sources, agencies, mine too. Harel/Markov no longer connected with my group; report anything to any you feel should know. I'll know where to find him if & when.*''

When he had read the note, Senator Taylor Bedford nodded once. Arising, he stepped over to the small marble-hearthed fireplace, struck a long, wooden match and lit a corner of the note. He held the blazing paper by one corner until it became imperative to let it go, then used the small brass shovel to thoroughly pulverize the ashes of it.

With his uncle's agreement to do his very best to acquire at least some federal funding for Project *feethami* and the senator's personal check for a midrange six-figure sum to tide his nephew over until dividend time arrived, James Bedford departed for his hotel. Tomorrow he would take his pictures and pitch to South Florida.

When he reached the street, however, his uncle's promised car had not arrived, so he approached one of the dozen or so well-armed guards, showed his permanent pass to the building and asked about the promised transport.

The guard, who wore the stripes of a sergeant, smiled. "Don't you worry none, Mr. Bedford, sir, he'll be here. See, that motor pool's a good half a mile away, and with this traffic the way it is—and it seems like it gets worser every minit of ever day of ever year, too—it's goin' to take him time for to get over here is all. A body's got to learn patience in D.C., anymore.

"You best get out there t'other side of the inside barriers, though, so's he can see you, sir."

Bedford wove his way out between the overlapping ranks of thick concrete blocks placed to prevent any vehicle larger than a two-wheeler from getting anywhere close to the front of the building. All similar buildings in the national and many state capitals had been thus protected since a spate of terrorist car and truck bombings several years before. No one to date seemed to know just who had ordered the bombings, though several different terrorist groups had claimed "credit" for them.

As he stepped between two of the outermost row of blocks, so as to be easily spotted by Sloan, his uncle's driver, a dark-blue, highly polished stretch limo slid smoothly to a stop before him to an ear-splitting screeching of tires and blatting of horns to its rear.

A red-faced man stuck his head and shoulders through an opening in the top of the sedan immediately behind the limo and shook a knobby, hairy fist, roaring, "Damn your whore's ass, you mutha! *Move* that long-ass fucker!"

But Bedford did not move, not an inch, for this was not Uncle Taylor's car; his was a lovingly rebuilt and refurbished antique, a Lincoln V-12 limousine, and this one was a Mercedes.

Abruptly, the nearest rear door opened and a broad-shouldered man with big, craggy features emerged to hold the door, gesture and say in accentless Standard American English, "Your car may well be an hour getting here, Mr. Bedford, and it looks like it may rain. Won't you share my car to your hotel?"

More and still more vehicles of all conceivable descriptions had joined the growing line behind the halted limo. Regardless of the almost solid line of traffic passing in fits and starts along the two outer lanes, vehicle after vehicle of the stalled lane was endeavoring to worm its way in among those still moving at all, their attempts accompanied by the sounds of still more screechings and honkings and shouts and the impacts of metal on metal now and then.

As Bedford stood and stared at his supposed benefactor, an utter stranger to him, he saw a bicycle messenger zip up between the halted line and the moving lane of vehicles. Obviously a young man who expected to die quite young, he thought.

A police traffic copter suddenly swooped in from somewhere behind; so low was the aircraft that only by dint of flattening himself against one of the flanking blocks of concrete did Bedford keep his feet in the powerful propwash.

The craft banked around and came back over, thankfully not so low on this pass, its loudspeaker booming, "DS Limo BU-20560-ND, you are blocking traffic. Resume forward movement at once, please. You must make another pass for your passengers. This is an urgent order. Move at once."

Bedford felt a tentative touch on his elbow and a voice to his rear said, "Mr. Bedford, sir, you better get in; 'less you do, the car'll have to go 'round agin."

Turning slightly, Bedford said, "Sergeant, this is not Senator Bedford's car, not the one he ordered for me, nor is this man any member of his staff."

"Is that so, sir?" said the sergeant, stepping past him in the direction of the halted limo and standing man. "And it ain't no car *I* recanize, either, come to think of it. A'right, mister, let's see some ID, and damn quick-like, too."

Making a movement toward one of the breast pockets of his dark suit coat, the standing man, smiling affably all the while, suddenly snapped his fingers, nodded wordlessly, then bent as if he might be reaching for something inside the rear compartment of the limo. But then, abruptly, he had stepped fully inside and slammed the door behind him, and the long vehicle was moving as fast as the traffic conditions would allow.

Pulling a communicator unit from his belt, the sergeant read off the numbers and letters stenciled on the rear of the limo's trunk as well as those on its license plate. After a moment, he thumbed up the screen protector, read what appeared on it, then whistled soundlessly.

"Mr. Bedford, sir, I'm goin' to have to ask you to come back inside with me, to our headquarters, downstairs. I think you just was about to be snatched by somebody for some reason, 'cause them D.C. vehicle numbers is s'posed to be on a five-ton truck and them Diplomatic Corps license plates was not an hour ago stole from the Thai Embassy along of the Toyota car they was on."

It all took some time. Senator Bedford was obliged to render his personal assurances in writing and seven copies worth of it to the effect that his bona fide blood nephew, James Bedford, was of sound mind, reliable judgment, and even temperament and was fully trained and proficient with firearms before the federal permit could be issued on a priority basis. Only when the card actually emerged from out of the machine in the building guardroom was he allowed to give James physical possession of the stainless PPK .380 caliber pistol and its two magazines of cartridges to stow in the shoulder harness under his coat.

With the guardroom officer's permission, he and his nephew were allowed to use one of the "safe rooms" of the facility—a room completely unmonitored by any source or agency, fully shielded against any sort of outside intrusion and constantly checked around the clock, every day, lest it be rendered unsafe.

Inside, Taylor Bedford threw his arms about his nephew and fiercely hugged him, saying, "God damn, boy, I'm glad you didn't just clamber into that damned car like too many other trusting souls might've done. How good a look did you get at the man who got out, eh? Did he speak with an accent? Could you tell what kind of accent it was?"

James shook his head. "No, Uncle Taylor, I think that's what made me suspicious, too; he had no accent at all, not even any regional patterns or inflections, he sounded just like a newscaster. How did he look? Oh, average height, but with broad, thick shoulders. The only things remarkable about his face were that he had big features and fairly wide cheekbones, a deep cleft in the chin and what looked like a short, sanded scar to the left side of it. He wore a dark suit, white shirt, tie of some subdued hue, shiny shoes; the clothes were American cut. I think his eyes were blue, his hair was brown and parted to the right, his face had a very light tan where glasses hadn't covered it, and that's about all I recall . . . oh, except that he was missing the first joint on the middle finger of his right hand. I told it all to that lieutenant out there before you got down here."

He paused, then asked, "You really think someone was trying to kidnap *me* for ransom?"

The senator shrugged, rubbed his forehead furiously with the heels of both hands, then shook his mane back into place before answering with another shrug. "Oh, hell, boy, it's possible, you know that as well as I do. But probable? No. In some backwater of another country, maybe, just maybe, but not smack in the middle of D.C., not in this day and time, no way.

"What did the man say, James, can you recall that?"

The younger Bedford closed his eyes, thought, then said slowly, " '*Mr. Bedford, your car may be as much as an hour getting here and it looks as if, . . . no, 'it looks like it may rain. Please share my car as far as your hotel.*' Or something like that, I think."

The senator nodded, grim-faced. "Clearly, then, the bastard was completely aware that I had rung up Sloan to come for you, knew what you looked like and knew that you would be bound for a hotel at which you had already booked a room. As I told you earlier, upstairs in my so-called private office, boy, every place in the whole district and beyond has become a fishbowl, a goddam sieve, every place except the few rooms like this one . . . and it is always just a matter of time before technology advances another notch or two and compromises even them. It—"

There was a knock on the outer door. The senator unlocked and opened the inner door, then unlocked the outer. There was a whisper that James could not hear, and without a word, his uncle went out, closing the outer door behind him. When he came back in, after four or five minutes' absence, he carefully closed and locked both doors before saying a word.

"James, immediately I heard about this business, I rang up some people, and that was them, calling on one of the guardroom's scrambler phones. James, your room and effects had been very professionally searched before they got there. Your room had had at least four surveillance devices recently installed in it, your luggage had been bugged and, as well, had been fitted with devices by which its movements could be tracked by anyone with compatible equipment. They removed everything, of course, but . . . but, boy, just what the hell have you gotten yourself into?"

"Have you had time to go over the files I left you, Uncle Taylor?" asked James, trying to ignore the cold chills racing up and down his back.

"No." The senator shook his leonine head. "I've got it stowed away in one of the few relatively safe places I know of around here—one of several special pockets I have my tailor put here and there inside my clothing."

"Okay, then," said James, "here's the gist of it." And once more he told the salient features of the story.

Chapter IX

The senator just regarded his nephew over steepled fingers for a while after the conclusion of the tale, facing him across the card-sized table in the safe room. At length he said, slowly, "Boy, you should go back to Idaho or wherever and just stay there until we get all this sorted out, you know. Will you? If I arrange for you to fly out tonight, will you do that . . . for me?"

James shook his head. "I can't, Uncle Taylor. I've some very important appointments in Dade County and other places. If you're able to get us funding and if the Japanese investors come through, fine, but we need money *now*. We've somewhat less than four million, as it sits, and that's simply not enough to tide us over until you or they can infuse bigger chunks of cash.

"That damned Harel/Markov is still costing us money, whether up there in the body or not. His precious yaks somehow knocked down enough Cyclone fencing to get loose on the higher end of the plateau, the whole pack of wisents followed them, and they all managed to make it down an almost vertical rock face into the woods down below without so much as a scratch, it would seem. Don't ask me or anybody else just how they all did it—maybe the bastard taught them how to levitate.''

The senator chuckled. ''Animals can do some truly remarkable things when they put their minds to it. James, you of all people should be aware of that. Don't you recall the story of Grandad's—your great-grandfather's—bay hunter? Of how he not only knew when the old man was near death, but got out of his paddock, into the house, up the stairs and into Granddad's bedroom, all sixteen-plus hands of him through a yard and house crowded with servants, relatives and nurses on a twenty-four-hour basis . . . and no single soul could later recall having seen him do any of it?

''Now I don't know spit about those wisents, other than that they look and act a lot like our native buffalo . . . bison, if you will . . . but I do recall having read somewhere that yaks are a mountain animal, even live high up in the Himalayan massif, so a puny little Rocky Mountain plateau was probably no obstacle—actually, more of a lighthearted romp to them.''

James grimaced and remarked, ''Well, that lighthearted romp of those bovids has already taken a sizable chunk out of what little the group had of existing funds and will take more before it's over and done. See, not only did they damage the fencing, they wandered around for a while near the plateau and then just seemingly disappeared from off the face of the earth. I had to hire on half a tribe of local Indians and actually put up cash bounties for their safe return before any of them turned up.''

''They were found, though, I take it?'' asked the senator.

James grimaced again. ''In a way, I wish they had really just disappeared from off the face of the globe, all things considered. Yes, they were found, but not by the

Indians. Twenty-odd crow-flight miles away, some state rangers who were on the lookout for poachers saw buzzards and rode into some very rugged country to find a dead bison bull—one of the forest bison, rare and so valuable, worse luck for our group.

"The beast was breathing his last and his wounds were acrawl with maggots, but even so it was easy for the rangers to see that he hadn't been done in by the hand of man but rather by another horned animal. They put him down with a bullet, took off his ID tag to turn in to the proper authority and set out to backtrack him, but had to turn back before they found what had been his herd.

"That night it started to rain, and it alternately rained, drizzled and threatened for three days, then came a weekend, so it was a total of five days before a larger number of men, with jeeps, horses and a chopper, went back up there to find what little the scavengers had left of the bull's carcass. The chopper it was finally located the herd—five bison cows, two calves, three wisent cows and a calf, one bull wisent that had been in a recent fight, and one yak cow.

"The wisent bull apparently had driven off the smaller, lighter yak bull while they all still were fairly close to the plateau area, because the yak took off in another direction, chanced across a pasture of a small dairy operation and decided this must be his new home and harem laid out for him. You can imagine the shock of the gentleman-rancher on finding a long-haired, long-horned and rather cantankerous wild bull among his prize cows; it's a wonder he didn't shoot the bastard out of hand, but he didn't.

"When we were passed word of where the escapee was, we went down there with the big truck and brought him back. But now the owner of the cows is rumbling about suing the group for probable damages to his purebred, prize-winning cows . . . and if he does, he'll probably win, be awarded a hefty settlement by any jury of locals, and we will be faced with the unhappy choice of either paying it or of paying more in the long run by going through the appeals process and, if we choose the latter, making local enemies we do not either need or want."

Taylor Bedford shrugged. "Settle out of court—that's the best way, I've found, in damage cases."

His nephew made a rude noise. "Tried. The bastard wants a truly stupendous sum, more than I think his entire hashup up there is worth, seems to be under the impression that we're a lavishly funded or endowed government project or, at least, a tax writeoff for some gigantic corporation or conglomerate. Gouging bastard!

"Even so, were that the only cost, I just might be able to do it, much as bowing to his demands would grate. But it's not. No, far from it. When the rangers found the wisents and the yak cow, they notified the project, of course, announcing that if we wanted any of them back alive, we had better get up there and get them out, pronto. Seems the wisent bull had taken the whole of his new-won herd up into an area that was almost inaccessible to even a horse. The big fucker had already injured one saddle horse and treed its rider for some hours, and the rangers were seemingly anticipating shooting him with some relish."

"So what did you do, James?" asked the senator.

His nephew sighed and cracked a knuckle. "Zeppy . . . Dr. Baronian and I jeeped up there, borrowed a brace of horses and rode up fairly close to the herd, then went in—very cautiously, mind you—afoot to find that the rangers were right about that big wisent bull being as mean as a Kodiak bear with a toothache, as murderous as a great white shark. He came close to getting us, too, he and the wisent cow with the calf. It was on our ride back to the jeep track that we two decided the only feasible way of getting the brutes out alive was by drug gun, cargo net and copter, and that's what we promised the rangers we'd do.

"Back at the project center, I phoned the outfit that had been providing us with copter services and explained the problem, and the next day, the president of the firm arrived aboard one of his smaller helicopters. He had been all smiles and cheery words when he first arrived—for after all, the group has been a really good, cash-on-the-barrelhead customer during our time up there—but after he had heard the details and had carefully studied the maps, seen exactly where he or one of his other pilots was going to have to take a copter large enough for the job—furthermore, take it up there and back for each of the animals—he became much cooler of manner and far more serious. After he had done some calculations, he came up with a figure that jarred me, nor would he budge from it, wouldn't come down one red cent, telling me in effect to take it or leave it, though offering the names of a few other copter services that might be willing to undertake the work.

"As I continued to try to haggle him down, he finally took my arm, walked me out to his copter, strapped me into it and then flew us both up to the area in question. Uncle Taylor, I've heard you and others—racing yachtsmen—speak in the past of 'living, prescient gales and storms,' but I never then knew, could not really picture, just what any of you meant by the phrase; well, I do now, please believe me, I do.

"That man is an exceedingly skillful copter pilot of many years experience, and I thank God for the fact, else

I'd likely not be here talking to you now. The winds up in those mountains, in and over the small, deep canyons we had to fly into, then lift out of, seemed to *know* just the best ways in which to see us crash into a wall of rock and seemed to do their utter damnedest to see us dead somewhere up there. I can't recall ever being so damned scared in my life, I mean it, every word of it.

"After that, after we'd gotten back safely to the project and I was outside a very stiff drink, I left the pilot nursing one of his own, met with the others in private and explained just how much the man was demanding for the services of his men and his copters, how hazardous was the area in which they would have to operate. I said that having flown in and out of there, I felt the astronomically steep price to be cheap, all things considered, did we feel it necessary to get those bovids out alive at all.

"Drs. Baronian and Marburg were of the opinion that we should just cut our losses there and then, and allow the rangers to put all the exotic strays down and, if nothing else, have a barbecue of wisent and yak up there. But, of course, Drs. Stekowski and Singh felt that as we had been responsible, at least in part, for having the animals imported to this area, we owed them all possible protection, whereupon Dr. Marburg took Dr. Stekowski's side and Dr. Baronian and I were outvoted.

"So I went out and signed a contract and gave over a check for a healthy deposit, then contacted the rangers—who, of course, would've been happiest had everything been done yesterday if not before—and we all went about setting up schedules, tentative ones, naturally, tricky as the weather can be that high up.

"The copter people got out the heavy-duty cargo nets they had used to transport some of the animals up to us with, before we'd acquired the big truck. Dr. Baronian and I tested the two carbon-dioxide-powered anesthetic rifles, and she carefully measured the doses for each syringe of dope. Then, on the appointed day, we jeeped back up there, rode and walked in, and put that damned killer of a wisent bull out first, then had to do the same for the nursing cow before we could even get close enough to wave in the copter and the men who'd help us get him in the net.

"To make a longish story a bit shorter, we did get all the big beasts out of that high canyon and back down to our plateau, though it ended up taking us two days and therefore costing us a good bit more, but that was the fault of the devilish weather and couldn't have been avoided. The only one we lost was that biggest wisent cow. Being sedated twice in two days was apparently more than her constitution could take, and she never woke up after she was back on the plateau, so I just had her skinned, dressed, butchered and hung . . . waste not, want not, you know. Besides, it was that much less flesh I had to buy for the cats, not to mention far fresher and far less likely to be full of chemicals and hormones."

"The native buffalo . . . ahh, bison, gave you no trouble, then?" asked the senator.

The younger man grinned. "Not really, no, though they did get into the way a lot, whenever the copter came in low and hovered. But, as the rangers explained, in really bad weather up there, the mountain bison herd is dropped bales of hay from choppers, so they've learned to associate the sounds of a low-flying or a hovering copter with food drops; they just thought it was chow time and were jockeying to be first in line. But compared to the damned wisents, the bison are almost tame as milk cows."

The senator nodded, smiling. Then, suddenly, he raised his eyebrows and snapped his fingers. "By the way, James, something you'd better know early on about that piece I gave you is this: the second, third and fourth round in each of those magazines is loaded with a very special bullet, a purple load."

"Purple load?" queried the younger.

"Explosive," replied his uncle. "Explosive on impact against anything hard, explosive very shortly after penetration of flesh or muscle. They're supposedly safe until fired and thereby armed—at least, so the manufacturer avers. Nonetheless, be very careful about dropping them or the magazine in which they're loaded, eh?"

James Bedford hissed between his teeth. "And this weapon came out of *your* private arsenal, Uncle? By God, you play hardball . . . and for keeps, don't you?"

A grim look came over the senator's patrician face. "James, you have spent precious little time in cities of past years, or you'd know whereof I speak. The entire megalopolis here, from Boston to Norfolk, is become a jungle. Even with police and security people thick as flies hereabouts, still there exists all too often a real need for self-protection if one appears at all affluent, and that is not even to mention the plots of one or another sort always bubbling somewhere in some embassy or terrorist group. Yes, I do have personal bodyguards, quite a few of them, but sometimes they might not be sufficient. Therefore I go armed, well armed, at all times and in almost all places, day and night. And now that it is made clear that some one has targeted you, you must quickly learn to emulate me in regard to self-protection.

"Furthermore, the problems never seem to improve, only to get worse and even worse, everywhere . . . and those are only the problems of which almost everyone is aware, things that can be easily seen, experienced, read in everyday life. There are other things, however, things of bone-chilling terror, which I am forbidden to impart to you or most people due to my security oaths, and seemingly there is nothing that the Congress, the Executive or any others can do to halt or even slightly ameliorate these things.

"My boy, I am deeply fearful. I am fearful that we now are living out the last days, weeks, months, possibly years of civilization as we know it. I feel a sense of foreboding, of an impending doom looming, glowering, gathering closer and ever more closely around us all . . . and I, I just feel so utterly helpless. With all my wealth, despite all my power, I feel completely alone sometimes, and as defenseless as a day-old baby. I can only pray that I be proved wrong."

Riffling back through the read pages until he found a date, Milo shook his head sadly. "No, you weren't wrong, Senator. Only a few more years prove your forebodings with a vengeance. And you were helpless to stop it, by then. Of course, no one will now ever know exactly who started that last, deadly exchange, not that it is of any importance; it just happened, and a whole world, billions of its people and ten thousand years' worth of cultural accretions, went down the tubes in mere weeks of elapsed time.

"The Russians of course thought we, the U.S., had started it, and we immediately assumed that they had, but from what little I was able to pick up over that powerful private radio setup, other persons around the world had other culprits in mind. A few of them suspected China, though how they could've gotten their relatively short-ranged missiles to points as far distant as Cairo and Rome or why they would've targeted such cities to begin, no one seemed able to imagine, not even their accusers.

"Some accused the Union of South Africa, too, but here again the distances and targets would've been unreal for South African equipment and motives. Not a few thought it to have been Cuba, but if so it was most odd that some of the earliest strikes were on a couple of far-southern Russian areas. The same is true as regards Iraq, too. Why would Iraq have struck at its longtime ally and armorer?

"A good deal of suspicion, from a good many quarters, fell on Israel, and with good reason. For decades, by then, they had been growling a nuclear-tipped threat at all their neighbors while their so-called Defense Forces gobbled up a bit of land here and a strip of land there from neighboring states for 'purely defensive purposes.' Had they for any reason or none at all come to feel threatened? Well, both their civil government and their military had full quotas of hotheads who could've launched at all real or imagined enemies. Others suspected India and/or Pakistan, too. But the weight of opinion was that it had been done by an aging, megalomanic Moslem dictator in North Africa—a man who had been so meddlesome and erratic over the years that even most of his own coreligionists had ended by virtually outlawing him and his country, and after a brief flirtation following his illegal seizure of power, not even the Kremlin or its satellites would have any more dealings with him than selling him military hardware for hard cash on the barrelhead. And what in hell could this United States senator have done to halt such an act of hatred and madness from so totally unexpected a quarter? What could anyone have done?

"And, sadder still, even if that one madman had been taken out of the world picture by some fortuitous happenstance prior to his final act of savage aggression, I'm dead certain that it would've been only a matter of time—likely a very short time, all things weighed and considered, at that—before one of the other suspects or yet another aggregation of fanatics or lunatics did the same thing.

"And, saddest of all, in the world political and military climate of that era—every nation of any power or aspiration armed to the teeth, treatied to the eyebrows, trusting the sworn words of neither allies nor enemies but fully expecting treachery at any moment, scared shitless of annihilation, yet determined to take any attacker down into death with it—what finally happened to the world and its people was a foreordained outcome, the worldwide nightmare of billions of folks for decades of time that became horrible reality overnight.

"By the time of Senator Taylor Bedford's tenure of office, it was become impossible for anyone to do anything to reverse the trends, save the nations from themselves, almost half a century too late. But my country, the one nation that could have done something to help set the other nations and nations then unborn, undreamed of, on a different, less destructive course, didn't; it let the brief chance slip by. The U.S. just let . . . hell, helped! . . . the juggernaut of global disaster start to roll, ignored by everyone until it had gained such momentum that no one, no nation or group of nations could've stopped it or even slowed it down.

"Eustace Barstow," he thought, his lips shaping the words, soundlessly, a horde of bitter memories welling up from below his conscious level, "General Eustace Barstow might, just might've been able to do something, there very shortly after the beginning of the thing, of that jugger-naut's roll that took so much of the world and its people down into dark disaster, doom, death.

"He recognized the menace, the true enemies of all freedom, of all civilization, early on, before World War Two even was concluded in Europe, but those who even took him seriously mocked him and his aims, called him 'superpatriot,' 'red-baiter' and much, much worse, most people just ignored him, wrote him off as some variety of looney-tune and forgot him. And I, more's the pity, espe-cially so as I had experienced firsthand just what the foe was capable of in pursuance of its selfish ends, deserted him too, got to hell away from him and the army and set about getting married and falling into a pisspotful of money I'd done nothing to earn or even deserve, a fine and loving woman I deserved even less and four children I adopted and reared as my own. And the end of it was suffering and death for all five of them and uncounted billions more, and all because none of us few who might've helped the even fewer who knew, who could look below the surface or into the future, if you will, and see what must be unless it could be quickly brought to a screeching halt, would do so.

"Eustace at least was able to keep his freedom, his status, his life, despite his lifelong efforts to fight the menace, to convert others to his beliefs. Some of the visionaries were not so fortunate. Rudolf Hess was impris-oned for nearly half a century, the last twenty-one years of it in what amounted to solitary confinement, until at last the poor old man hanged himself. General George Patton, unabashable, suffered an auto 'accident' that proved fatal. Others, like Ezra Pound, were locked away for years in madhouses and there subjected to the spate of twentieth-century tortures known as 'behavior modification' or were rendered intellectually impotent through means of icepick lobotomies. Most were simply pressured or ridiculed into silence.

"Oh, if only I . . ."

A brace of his uncle's bodyguards collected James Bedford's luggage and effects and they arrived at the senator's tightly guarded suburban residence at almost the same time as the elected legislator and his guest. James had been to the house in times past, but only for meals or small, informal gatherings.

While they had awaited the senator's copter on the roof of his office building, he had said, "You could've been put up in one of the so-called security-guest areas of several of the bigger hotels in town, but security is relative in such places, I've found; why, only last month one of those wild-eyed terrorist types got into one of them long enough to thoroughly kill a Turkish businessman before being cut almost in half at the waist by a guard's machine pistol."

James Bedford sighed. "Armenian or Greek, this time?"

The senator shrugged. "Neither . . . that is so far known. No, the perp had jumped a ship in Baltimore Harbor two weeks before, a Turkish-registered ship, at that. But, clearly, someone or some group had brought him here, hidden him, armed him, briefed him, gotten him into and up there. The only certain thing is that he'll never be persuaded to tell us anything now.

"No, the security-guest thing is obviously fallible, as full of holes as the proverbial Swiss cheese. My place, on the other hand, is about as safe as anyplace can be these days—protected by state-of-the-art equipment and a small but well-trained staff. Hell, James, it would take the likes of a platoon of air cavalry to get into the place, and even then they'd know damned well that they'd been in a fight.''

Over dinner, the elder Bedford said, ''Actually, I should've thought to invite you out here, overnight, anyway; I don't see enough of any of the family anymore, it seems, and, between mistresses as I currently am, there's no one to talk to out here except servants or bodyguards. I don't suppose I could persuade you to phone and reschedule your appointments, then stay over until one of the agencies determines just who was trying to snatch you and why, could I?''

Chewing industriously at a gobbet of octopus, James could only shake his head.

The senator nodded. ''I thought not, but it was worth a try to me.'' His voice sounded a bit sad and wistful.

Finally swallowing, James asked, ''What happened to . . . Sidonia, was it? She was your most recent, wasn't she?''

His uncle smiled. ''No, you're a bit out of date. Sidonia met and wed an Argentine chap, that was almost two years ago; I gave her away at the ceremony, in addition to paying for her trousseau and for the minor surgical procedure that restored her hymen.''

''That did *what*?'' James burst out, almost dropping his salad fork.

''Restored Sidonia's hymen, my boy, gave her the semblance of virginity for her wedding night. You or I wouldn't've given much of a damn, of course, but to certain cultures, such things are still extremely important,'' Taylor Bedford replied before forking half a cherry tomato and a soupçon of greens into his mouth.

"Where in hell did she meet this antique gentleman?" asked James. "At a meeting of the Neanderthal Society?"

Chewing, Taylor wrinkled his brows in thought, swallowed, then shook his head. "Never heard of a Neanderthal Society, James, but then we both have our own narrow fields of specialities. No, I believe they met at some charity function of the Roman Catholic diocese. I think that was it."

James snorted. "Figures. Saint Sidonia the Retreaded Virgin. So, how many came after her, Uncle?"

"Only one, James, a young woman who called herself Deirdre and claimed to be French-Danish . . . but wasn't. She and her employers had gone to great lengths to cover her well and very deeply, and she was basically a nice girl, I think; at least I was already becoming rather fond of her when I was presented with more than enough evidence that I had been, in effect, nurturing a potential viper in my bosom. Bringing her into the city and turning her over for interrogation—with all that I know about those procedures— was one of the most difficult things I ever have had to do. And, in the end, it was all for nothing; she managed to remove a false tooth and bit into the cyanide capsule it contained before her interrogation had gotten beyond the stage of threats and the presentation of before-and-after photos of previous suspects." Infinite sadness was evident in the older man's tone and eyes.

"Oh, you poor bastard," said Milo aloud and with sincere feeling, reading the words in the journal of the younger Bedford, there in that underground lamplit room, so many scores of years after the deaths of both the Bedfords and most of humanity. "You poor, poor old bastard."

Abruptly, his memory dredged up the scene in the dusty camp—that nameless security installation somewhere in the Commonwealth of Virginia in 1946. Holding in his arms the just-dead body of the Russian woman who had called herself Betty, the woman whom he had begun to love, the woman with whom he had sexed bare hours before, the woman from whose open lips arose the bitter-almond reek of cyanide.

It had been in the aftermath of that terrible morning that he had left the operation headed up by Eustace Barstow. "I told him and myself that I was just tired of watching people die. Little did I know then just how much more dying would be brought about by the defection from his terribly important cause of me and people like me. And by the early seventies, by which time I knew, it was really too late for him or an army of hims to do anything that would've done anyone any good. And that's just about what he told me that night in my hotel room, right after I was brought back from 'Nam, too."

Staring at the ice he was swirling around in his glass, the general officer in mufti had said sadly, "Thank you for the offer, Milo, but you made it about a quarter century too late. Had I had you and a few others even as late in the game as 'forty-eight or 'forty-nine . . . who knows? But now? Well, as one of my wives used to say, 'Too much water has gone over the bridge.' "

He had thrown down the drink, placed the glass on the table and fixed Milo with a stare. "Now, my friend, the world is bound irrevocably for hell in the proverbial bucket. Only a true miracle will stop it, and I've no faith in miracles. When will it happen? Well, it could be happening, the incident that will set off our *Götterdämmerung*, even as we two sit here tonight, but I rather doubt it, really. No, I give a minimum of twenty years and it might even go on as long as fifty years before we have true hell on this earth. But fifty is the maximum. Neither of us will live to see it, thank God.''

Remembering, Milo thought, "How wrong he was. I didn't live to *see* much of it, true, but I heard about it from points all over the globe on that radio. And what little I did actually witness was pure hell and no mistake.''

The general had continued, "No, Milo, the time is now long past when you could help me or I could help anyone . . . almost. But I still owe you, owe you more than I could ever repay, really, and I still have a fairly good, fairly effective and powerful organization with which I can help you . . . if you'll let me.'' The officer stood, stepped across the room and built himself yet another drink, then turned and took his seat on the edge of the bed once more.

Milo had just shaken his head. "General, I can't think of how you could help me or exactly why I would need your help . . . or that of anybody else, for that matter. Look, the very worst that any of these leftist liberals could do would be to cashier me, throw me out of the army without a pension, maybe with a DD, though I doubt any of them would dare go so far, not in the case of a career officer who's been through three damned wars. Even on the far-outside chance that this McGovern wins, no new administration is going to want to start off its hegemony with that kind of a stench to dog it through the next four years.

"And even in the worst scenario, General, the last things I need are a pension and VA benefits to sustain me. Did you forget? Another general, my late buddy, Jethro Stiles, left me heir to an obscene amount of money and possessions. Yes, I'd miss the army after so many long years in it, but I sure as hell won't starve or be anything approaching impoverished, not if I live another hundred years.''

"You're most likely right about things, Milo,'' said Barstow, tiredly. "Nonetheless, I'll see that the skids are greased well for you, see that you get the kind of send-off your years of loyal service if nothing else merit you.'' When Milo opened his mouth, Barstow waved a hand, saying, "No, no protests, my old friend. It will be no slightest trouble for me and mine, and, moreover, it will give me the chance and the great pleasure to jam a handful of stinging nettles up certain hemorrhoidal left-liberal arses over there in the puzzle factory, then be serenaded by the sweet music of their shrieks of outrage and agony.

"But I'll also be leaving you a card on which will be some telephone numbers and a couple of addresses for me. When, if, you ever need me, need any help I can give, call or wire or write me. Please promise me, Milo.''

Milo was vouschafed less than a week to enjoy wearing the silver eagles of his full-colonelcy before they were replaced with the single stars of a brigadier general, and within yet another week he was officially retired. After a brief trip to New York City and a few days spent with the aging attorney who had handled most of his affairs for a quarter century, he purchased a new automobile and drove back down through New Jersey, Maryland and the District of Columbia into northern Virginia. In no rush to get anywhere for any purpose, he drove in a leisurely manner, enjoying the sights of a peaceful, undevastated countryside, roads that might own a few potholes here and there but no shell craters, streets with green lawns upon which well-fed children played children's games.

Lulled by the steady throb of the big automobile's powerful eight-cylinder engine, he rolled along highways between fields of growing crops and pastures on which grazed sleek cattle or leggy, well-bred horses, with nowhere a rusting carcass of a tank or APC or SP-gun, no burned-out trucks or shattered jeeps' hulks.

It was an intensely soothing trip for him and he deliberately strung it out, made it last, driving only so far as he wished each succeeding day, then finding a place to stay each night—tourist court, motel or real hotel, whatever was available at the time and the place and took his fancy of the moment.

He dined simply or elegantly or not at all in the same mode as he lodged, dependent mostly upon what facilities were there, were available wherever he decided to stop—Nabs and Cokes, hot dogs or hamburgers with french fries and malteds, chow mein and beer, Chateaubriand and vintage wines, all were the same to him and all were equally enjoyed in an unhurried manner, for he felt—to use the old-army expression—that he had the rest of his life to do this in . . . though he could not then have imagined just how long the rest of his life was to be.

Other than the various potables consumed with his meals, Milo drank very little on the protracted trip down from New York to Virginia. Nor was his near-abstinence because he did not like spirits or lack a head for them, he just felt a need to see and feel what he saw and felt unaffected by drugs or stimulants.

Benighted somewhere on the road from Baltimore to the District, he found himself seated in a bar enjoying a preprandial couple of whiskies before walking next door for dinner. While the paunchy bartender slowly polished glasses, most of the other patrons—clearly locals—sipped

draft beer and watched the news on the television fitted
into the paneled wall above the bartender's bald head.

Concentrating on enjoyment of the pleasant burn, the
smoky fumes of the alcohol in mouth and gullet, Milo did
not at first hear the man who stood before him, beyond the
shiny bar.

"Ready for another'n, sir?" smiled the bartender, with
a real diffidence, for damned few of his customers were in
the habit of ordering double Chivases, much less tipping
handsomely with the service of each drink.

Milo glanced down at the small swallow or so of whis-
key left in the old-fashioned glass and shrugged. "Why
not? Yes, one more, please."

As the bartender approached with the fresh drink, the
outer door opened and a slight young man entered and
limped up to the bar a few feet down from Milo, at whom
he smiled and nodded in a polite manner. The man appeared to be in his twenties. In addition to the limp, his
face and the backs of his hands were covered with shiny
scar tissue. Milo had seen that kind of scarring before,
over the years, and could make a pretty shrewd guess as to
just what had caused it.

Spying the newcomer, the bartender's thick lips moved
in an almost soundless "*Oh, shit*," and he hurriedly glanced
back at the knot of locals grouped before the television,
but as they were rapt by the medium, he set the glass
before Milo with a flourish, accepted the payment and tip
with a smile and a nod, then passed swiftly down to lean
as far as his belly would let him across the bar toward the
scarred man.

"Gawddammit, Billy," Milo heard him urgently whisper, "won't what Bubba done to you the lastest time
enough? He ain't seed you yet, so get to hell out, 'fore he

does. Mist' Chamberlin, he ain't over here to drag Bubba and them off of you t'night, an' by the time I could get the cops out here, you'd be dogmeat, and you knows it, too. Please, just leave, huh?''

But it was too late.

"Hey!" Milo heard a nasal voice ring from up the bar. "Hey, y'awl, look who's here. The fuckin' baby-burner's done come back to finish gettin' his lumps. I got dibs on bashin' the fucker first. Who wants to hol' him for me, huh?''

Chapter X

Rocking slightly from the amounts of beer he had poured down his throat since he had gotten off work at the sand and gravel quarry, the big, rawboned man stalked up the bar, his fists clenched and cocked, the light of joyful sadism shining from his pale, bloodshot eyes.

"Now, goddammitall, Bubba," the bartender half-shouted, "you and them leave Billy alone, you hear? He's a disabled vet'run, he cain't fight you even was you to fight fair, one on one, and you knows it, too."

"You jest tend to your own fuckin' bizness, Chester," said the big man, echoed by the two now coming in his wake. " 'Lest we hev to whup your fat ass, too. Thet lil gal I useta fuck down in D.C., she tol' me all bout these fuckin' baby-burners and all. And I ain't gone have none the fuckers drinkin' in any bar I drinks in, hear?

"You know how poorly I was for a long time, how plumb bad I felt when the fuckin' jarheads wouldn't take a big whole man like me, but took that gawdam little skinny pissant of a fuckin' half-breed injun, there? The fuckers, they said I was somethin' like moshunly unstable or suthin'. But I'm fuckin' glad them bastids didn't take me, now, 'r the fuckin' army neither, too, 'cause then they'd be calling me a fuckin' baby-burner, too.''

The bartender headed purposefully toward the far end of the bar, one hand in a pocket that jingled with change. But one of the two following the instigator turned, anticipating, and ripped the wire of the coin phone's handset loose from the box. Grinning at the thus-stymied bartender, he headed back toward the helpless victim awaiting them.

Standing, Milo stepped into the path of the trio of toughs. "If you're so anxious to use those knuckles, you overgrown ape, why not try them on a man closer to your size, a man who isn't crippled and can fight you back? Or do you lack the guts? No wonder the army and the marines wouldn't accept you, you oversized, gutless cretin," he remarked in a conversational tone, smiling the while.

"You git the hell out'n my way, mister," ordered Bubba, his face reddening with anger. "I'll stomp you soon's I'se done with this fuckin' baby-burner. I'll stomp your ass good, too."

"Just what is your moronic definition of 'baby-burner,' you pig?" demanded Milo, still smiling and seemingly friendly, "Or have you ever troubled your pea-brain enough to define it?"

The big man stopped then, still red-faced and with clenched, cocked fists, but now with his forehead wrinkling up. "Wal, it's like thet gal I useta fuck down ta D.C. useta say, enybody as was in the in . . . naw, unjust war over to Vietnam was bound to be one them damn baby-burners, what burnt up lil babies alive jest for fun."

"And you never once wondered at whether or not this nameless woman was telling the truth or even was of sound mind? Consider, any woman who would willingly have sex with such a thing as you would have to be a mental basket case, as emotionally unstable as the Marine Corps and U.S. Army found you to be, you hulking lunatic," said Milo, ignoring what sounded like a low moan from the fat, trembling bartender.

Milo's friendly smile suddenly became a mocking grin as he asked, "Or did she actually have sex with you at all, Bubba? I, for one, would doubt it. Things like you usually have three kinds of sex: what you buy from cheap whores, what you think about and what you talk about, generally out of the whole cloth, the lies that lead others to think you far more of a man than you really are or will ever be.

"So, isn't that it, Bubba? Didn't you lie about this little gal in D.C.? Or was it really a little boy, eh? The men who talk the most about their vast and varied female conquests amazingly often turn out to be closet faggots. Is that what you are, Bubba? Do you get your jollies going to dark moviehouses on Saturday afternoons to jerk off little boys in the dark? Isn't that the—"

With a roar of pure rage from a wide-open mouth in a livid face that also now contained eyes filled with bloodlust, the huge man swung a big, knobby fist at Milo's mocking face. Milo easily ducked the roundhouse swing and, as the man's own force spun him half about, gave him the toe of one shoe in the right kidney.

The roar abruptly became a gasping whine of agony, and that was when the man who had disabled the telephone slipped behind Milo and held him with a full nelson, crowing, "I got the fucker now, Bubba. You and Abner paste him good."

The one called Abner, almost as big as the still-suffering Bubba, made to do as bid, but Milo—using the support of the man who was holding him—slammed both feet with all his force into the midriff of the advancing attacker, sending him tumbling back onto one of the tables, which collapsed under his weight. An elbow in his erstwhile captor's ribs quickly freed him of any restraint and left him ready to eagerly meet the recovered Bubba with enough of his best antique, bare-knuckle boxing blows to send him back bloody and reeling until he tripped over the still-retching Abner and crashed down atop both him and the wrecked table.

"*Gawdam you, you muthafuckuh*!" yelled the man who had been trying to hold him for a beating. "I'll fix yo' ass!"

Milo whirled to find the man holding a barstool above his head. Reaching up with both hands, he caught and held the unwieldy weapon while stepping close enough to knee-lift the man. Gurgling, his eyes looked to pop from out their sockets, the man let go the barstool to sink down onto the floor, holding his crotch and gagging.

Seeing this, the three locals still seated up the bar all stood and turned purposefully toward Milo, looks of grim determination on their unshaven faces.

Turning his head toward the scarred man, Milo said hurriedly, "Gyrene, get to hell out of here. Go next door and tell them to get the cops here before I have to kill somebody."

The scarred man shook his head. "You the one better get out of here, buddy. And you don't want any part of no cops, either, not around here, leastways. That bastid whose balls you just rearranged, he's the sher'ff's younger brother. It's Sher'ff Chamberlin owns thishere bar, you know."

Then there was no time for talking. Having been witness to all that had so quickly befallen their friends, the three men spread out as widely as the space permitted, to come at Milo from three directions but more or less concerted.

"Field expedients," Milo muttered as he picked up the double shot still untasted and flung the strong whisky accurately into the eyes of the closest attacker, then hurled the thick-bottomed glass at the one farthest away. The middlemost man came in at an uncertain crouch, chin tucked behind left shoulder, fists held low . . . and Milo savate-kicked him long before he could reach jabbing distance, following the left foot to the belly with a right foot to the face that sent the man stumbling for a moment before he sprawled backward, his head hitting the floor with a solid, painful-sounding thump.

The splash of whisky had rendered its target entirely *hors de combat*; he was leaning against the bar rubbing at his eyes and alternately moaning and shrieking that he was blinded.

But the third and largest man, despite a heavily bleeding cut under one eye from the hurled glass, had brought out from someplace about his person a big jackknife, opened it and was coming toward Milo at a knife fighter's crouch, muttering under his breath something concerning "damnyankee chit'lins all over the floor."

"I just may have to hurt this one seriously," thought Milo. "The fucker looks like he knows what he's doing, has done it all before." Stepping away from the bar, he glanced down to be sure of his footing. He knew of old just how much knife wounds hurt, and he did not care for another.

The fat bartender had disappeared, at least Milo could not see him anywhere, though he could not have gotten out the only visible door without having been seen.

Both moving cautiously on flexed legs, Milo and the knifeman circled each other warily, slowly drawing incrementally closer one to the other. The man held his empty left hand out, ready to strike or grab or claw, but the right fist holding the shiny honed blade stayed safely down just below his hip level, winking now and again as it reflected errant beams of light. Although his lips moved from time to time, he made no threats, and this worried Milo, for he well knew the implicit dangers of silent fighters.

Both rapt in the deadly dance, neither man's mind registered the shrieking of tires in the parking lot or even the stomping of heavy feet up to the door, not even the opening of that door with some force. But only a deaf man could have ignored the baritone roar of unquestioned authority from the doorway.

"Damn your ass, Doug, you drop that knife this minnit or I'll crease your thick skull again like I done last time. You *hear* me, you fucker you?"

As the knife clattered onto the floor, Milo first extended a leg to kick it from out the easy reach of its owner, then turned about to confront the man at the door.

The man in the khaki uniform was taller than Milo and big, bigger even than the now groaning Bubba. Below an iron-grey brush cut and trimmed eyebrows of a slightly darker hue, his face was craggy . . . and oddly familiar, though Milo could not call up a name to go with it, just then. His nose was canted and a little flattened, while the knuckles of the hand that gripped the highly polished billy club were extensively scarred. A gleaming holster was secured to an equally gleaming Sam Browne belt and held a big revolver; a five-pointed star that gleamed like pure gold was pinned over the big man's heart.

"Who the hell are you, mister?" he demanded of Milo. "What the hell you mean comin' into *my* bar in *my* county and beatin' up on a bunch of *my* customers and friends?"

Before Milo could answer, the former Marine spoke up.

"It's my fault, Sher'ff. Bubba and Abner and your brother, Wally, they was setting for to hurt me agin and this gentleman, he got up and took them on his own self is all."

"Wally?" demanded the lawman, taking another long step into the room. "Where's my brother, Wally? What'd he do to Wally?"

Hearing his name repeated, the unshaven man looked up from where he still crouched in agony, half propped against the bar, his eyes swimming and his day's growth of stubble wet with tears, his chin still dripping vomitus onto his now soaked and filthy shirt. "Sher . . . Sherwood," he gasped, sobbing, "thishere fucker, he kneed me, kneed me raht in the bawls, too . . . and . . . and I thank he done busted one my ribs, too. Bash him, bash him good."

"Did you do whut my brother claims you done to him, mister?" demanded the lawman, slowly raising his billy, his blue eyes now cold and hard-looking as agates.

Milo shrugged "Sheriff, I had no option, no choice; it was either let him smash a barstool over my head, kill him, or hurt him enough to put him down for a while. Would you rather I'd killed him, then? And I hereby serve you fair warning, too: while I own the greatest respect for legally designated authority, you try to use that baton on me and I'll clobber you, too." He said it all bluntly, matter-of-factly and with patent sincerity.

"Who the hell are you, anyway, mister?" snapped the lawman. "You got guts, I'll say thet much, you got you ten miles of guts, to take on a half a dozen the toughest brawlers in the whole county, then offerin' to go after me, too. Seems to me I seen you somewhere, heard you, too. What's yore name? Whatall do you fer a livin', huh?"

"My name is Milo Moray," answered Milo. "I'm a retired army officer."

"Wal, gawdam-I-rackun!" the lawman swore feelingly. "I's in the army during the World War Two with a captain name of Milo Moray. You mus' be, got to be his son."

It suddenly all clicked together, into place and proper order in Milo's mind. "No, I'm not my son, Master Sergeant Chamberlin, I'm me, Milo Moray. I was your platoon sergeant, then your platoon leader, then your company commander, before I got transferred to an operation in Munich, back in 'forty-five."

The lawman just stared, goggle-eyed for a moment, then he declared, "Milo? Hell, no, you cain't be Milo, the old sarge. Man, he was as old's I wuz or some older, and didn't look no older then then you do now, mister. So you his son, really, and jest been tryin' to josh me, right?"

It took some doing, quite a bit more facts and dredged-up incidents and long-forgotten names of men living and dead, but at last Milo won Sheriff Sherwood Chamberlin's full belief as to his identity. Tears in his eyes, the big lawman impulsively lapped his long, brawny arms about his old comrade-in-arms and hugged him with a strength of which a grizzly would not have been ashamed.

Stepping back, dabbing embarrassedly at his eyes with his big knuckles, he all at once became again aware of the sprawled and still or moaning, bleeding men lying on the scuffed, stained floor amid smashed furniture. "Chester?" he shouted. "Chester, you go nex' door and tell Sampson I said to call the fuckin' rescue squad. Tell the fuckers I said best send two meat wagons, anyhow."

Looking up at his elder brother, the man Milo had kneed swallowed a sob, then whined petulantly, "You ain't gone bash him, are you, Sherwood? All he done done to

me, yore own baby brother, and you ain't gone bash him
evun oncet, are you?''

Leaning over, the lawman reached out for a handful of
his brother's shirt, thought better of it and instead grasped
him by his lank, greasy hair, growling, "No, I ain't,
Wally, 'cause you had it comin', see. I 'spect you had it
comin' more'n just oncet, too, whin I bashed mens for
you. You keep follering the lead of that crazy, no-count
Bubba, you gone wind up daid, someday soon. Hear
me?''

From beside the door, the fat bartender piped up, "Won't
none Bubba's fault, this time, Sher'ff. That damn swell,
he stuck his nose in where won't none his bizness, see.
And he said plumb terr'ble things to my pore cousin
Bubba, too. He called him some really common things,
said he went to the movies and all jest to jack off lil boys
is all. And—''

"Gawdam you anyhow, Chester,'' roared the lawman,
"dint I jest thishere minnit git th'ough tellin' you whut to
go do? You don't go do whutall I tol' you, you gone need
another meat wagon all to yorese'f. Hear me?''

While they awaited the arrival of the rescue squad, the
sheriff went from casualty to casualty, squatting beside
each of them and critically examining their injuries, com-
menting upon them. "Damn, Milo, you done some kinda
first-rate fuckin' job on ole Bubba, here; he ain't dead,
don't worry none about that, he's jest done passed out agin
is all. Two, mebbe three, his front tooths is gone, broke
off, it's purely a wonder you dint cut the holy livin' fuck
outen your knuckles, too. His damn nose is broke for sure
and his jaw may be, too, and you can bet your fuckin' ass
his cheekbones is cracked all to hellangone. Tomorra, he
gone look like Sam Potter's whole fuckin' herd of cows

run over him . . . probly feel like it, too. Mebbe it'll take some the meanness outen him for a while, but don't put no money on't.''

Ungently, he proded at his brother's thorax with the tip of his billy until he produced a thick scream of pain. He nodded, then, ''Yup, Wally's got one, mebbe two cracked ribs; too bad won't his fuckin' shithead. Now, Wally, I done tol' you time after time to keep 'way from that fuckin' looney Bubba Rigny, ain't I? He's got the kinda crazinesses rubs off on other people, and sometime me or somebody is gonna have to kill him and, like as not, some of whoever's with him then, too. I don't want one them to be my baby brother, Wally, is all. If you'd minded me 'fore this, you wouldn't be there covered in puke with cracked ribs and a dang ball-big fulla scrambled eggs atween yore legs, neither.

''Jerry,'' he admonished the man in whose face Milo had flung the whisky, ''you ain't gone go blind jest 'cause you got likker in yore eyes. But you don't stop rubbin' and clawin' at 'em, you jest might wind up with a white cane and a *po*-lice dawg, yet.''

As he moved on to squat by another body, his peripheral vision registered the sly movement toward the door of the knife fighter, and he commented warningly, ''Doug Wilkes, I ain't give you leave for to go, yet. You get your sad ass back here and put it in a fuckin' chair, till I says diffrunt. I have to come after you, you gone wish I'd let Milo here work on you, too.''

Lifting the head of an unconscious man by its dirty red hair, he used calloused fingertips to explore the egg-sized lump on the back of it, grunted, then let it go to thump back on the hard floor, turning his attention to the swelling, already-discolored face. ''Milo, what the fuck you

clobber Eugene Fitzger'ld here with, enyhow, a fuckin'
maul? He's another good ole boy's gone be drinkin' his
fuckin' beer th'ough a fuckin' straw for a while, I figgers.
Thanks to you, old buddy, things is gone be dang quiet
and peaceful round abouts thishere county till this bunch
gets done healin' up, I'd say. Layin' here is five the
bigges' troublemakers I got to plague me : . . an' it's
gone be six if one Doug Wilkes don't quit tryin' to snag
thet fuckin' knife with his fuckin' toe.''

Still not looking around, he said, ''Billy, take the cuffs
outn the pouch on the back of my belt here, and put 'em on
Doug; cuff him to that chair, he ain't trustable. Then step
out to my cruiser and git Hannibal on the radio, hear? Tell
him I said for to send car number three over here and pick
Doug up, book him for ADW and th'ow him in the fuckin'
lockup there to wait on Judge Daniels. He done drawed
that fuckin' fancy-ass spic shiv of his one time too many,
to my way of thinkin'. I think some time on the road
gang'd make a whole world of diffrunce in him.''

With the prisoner securely cuffed and sitting glumly in
the chair, Chamberlin, still at a squat, turned to face Milo
and said, ''Damn, but I wish I could git that boy, Billy
Crawford, to come to work for me, be one my deppities.
He come back from Vietnam with a whole pisspot full of
medals, you know, and he allus was a real bright boy, and
Lord knows he could use the money, too, him and his lil
wife. But he ain't got him but one and a half legs, no
more, see, and he says he might not be able to do ever'thing
a whole depity could do, and he's proud, won't take
nothin' looks like no kind of char'ty. But if I had a real
sharp boy like Billy to run the desk and office and all, I
could put that cornball shitheaded Hannibal out in one the

cars and . . ." He broke off as the slight man limped back into the bar.

"Sher'ff," said the scarred man, "Depity Gregory said that he'd get a car here as quick as he could and he said to tell you he couldn't find no paper on anybody named Milo Moray, neither."

"Who the hell ast him to?" demanded Chamberlin, his craggy face darkening. "*I* needs wants and warrants, it'll be *me* asts for wants and warrants!"

The scarred man shuffled a bit uneasily. "Well . . . he did say Chester had been on yore car radio to him . . . ?"

Chamberlin nodded shortly. "Figgers. Bubba's his cousin and he didn' like watchin' him get beat to a frazzle here. But it none of it wouldn't of come down if he'd done like I tol' him and jest kept Bubba and his crowd of fuckers outen thishere bar of mine. Wal, Mr. Chester's done had the course, this time 'round, that's for sure, that's for dang sure. I'll have Sampson find me a new bartender as ain't a fuckin' relative of nobody in this county, and Chester can start workin' off his fuckin' fat ass and beergut out the gravel pits agin.

"Oh, speakin' of Sampson, Billy, would you step over there and tell him to set up the private room for me and you and Milo to have dinner in tonight? Tell him steaks and lobsters. That sound a'right to you, Milo?"

Later, seated across the table from Chamberlin in the lavishly appointed private dining room of the restaurant, sipping whisky and packing his old, battered pipe, Milo asked, "What ever happened after I left the company, the battalion, there in Delitzsch? Did you all really get into the Bavarian Alps to hunt SS?"

"Aw, naw, Milo." Chamberlin shook his head, his cornpone speech lessening noticeably, for some reason.

"Seems like the minnit the fuckin' war ended, ever SS and Nazi and his fuckin' brother was doin' his fuckin' damnedest for to get the hell out of Germany or elst cover his ass so it looked like he hadn't never been nothing but a pore, rear-rank private or *Gefreite* or suthin' in the fuckin' Wehrmacht or a swabby in the Kriegsmarine or best a pore fuckin' civilian. Them *Oberkommando* bugtits might've set plans to fight up there to the last bullet, but with old Hitler dead, won't nobody was willin' to do no such thing when push come to shove. So the battalion jest squatted right where we was for a while, gettin' fat and sassy on hot A-rations and all the hootch we could find to liberate, getting in replacements and equipment and all, learnin' what it felt like to be clean and wear clean clothes agin, standing chickenshit inspections ever now and then and even doing fuckin' close-order drill, for Chrissakes, and route marches and compass problems, too.

"Right after you left, that fuckin' John Saxon, he twisted my pore balls some kind of fierce till I let him commission me, then upped me to first looey and give me the comp'ny. He done the same thing to Bernie Cohen and made him my exec. That horny old bastid was a piss-cutter, he was, God bless his old soul."

"John's dead, then?" asked Milo sadly. "Do you know when, Chamberlin, or how?"

The lawman nodded. "Yeah, happens I do, Milo. The official version goes that while he was at some kinda conference in Paris, he died of a heart attack in his sleep one night."

"And the unofficial story?" prodded Milo.

Despite his solemnity, Chamberlin could not repress a grin. "John was a BG, by then, you know, and he and a bunch of other division officers had done gone down to

Paris to whoop it up some. Story goes, John died in bed, a'right, but not in his damn sleep, not no way. His heart gave out while he was humpin', hot-shaggin' some French whore, he was. Died in the saddle, he did, and if you gotta go, damn if that ain't the way to go—chock full of good food and strong booze and balls-deep inside of a redhot pussy. Bernie and me thought old John would've chose that way, if it'd been for him to choose, you know.''

"What about Bernie?'' asked Milo, his clearest memory of the man being the sight of him belly-crawling out of the company CP on the day the Hitler Jugend snipers killed Jethro Stiles and Sergeant Webber, with a carbine, a bazooka and two rockets for it.

Chamerlin shrugged. "He made out real good, Milo. Back as early as the first, real Sixtieth Division reunion, back in 'fifty-five, he was running one his fambly's two men's stores in Richmond, Virginia. He went back and really did marry that lil gal he all the time was talkin' about, and by 'fifty-five, he had him five kids and anothern on the way. I didn't get to no more of the reunions till the big one, down to D.C., back in 'sixty-two, and by then Bernie'd done parlayed his two stores into near twenny in three states and had got to nine kids before him and his wife had figured enough was enough. We ain't seen each other since then, we use to write to each other now and then, but I jest ain't got no time anymore, with all the pies I got my fingers into, and I guess he don't either.''

It was at that point that the scarred man—who had insisted on phoning up a neighbor with a phone, then had had to wait while his wife was fetched to talk to him—returned to the room, saying, "Sher'ff, Depity Fontaine wants you to call him and so does Dr. Kilpatrick over to the hospital.''

With a brusque "Thank'y, Billy; be back fast as I can, Milo," the big man departed.

Sipping at a beer—he did not smoke and had politely declined any of the whisky—Billy Crawford proved a veritable fountain of information about Sheriff Sherwood Chamberlin, and there was, Milo soon became aware, much to tell of his sometime comrade-in-arms.

"My paw and Sher'ff Chamberlin, they come back to the county from the war 'bout the same time, Mr. Moray, sir. They both went back to work out to the gravel pits, but the sher'ff, he didn't stay long, for all that Mr. Royal, hisself, offered for to up his pay and make him a supervisor if he would stay. Naw, he moved down to D.C. and went on the cops, there, found out he liked cop work and commenced at taking college courses in it.

"He'd married Betty Watling within a year of coming home, but she just couldn't seem to get to like living in D.C., so he took a little house out on Yellow Creek Road for her and come out here as often as he could to be with her. Long about 'fifty-two or -three, I think it was, old Sher'ff Quinn, his car blowed a tire on a wet road and rolled over three, four times and burnt up with him in it.

"He'd been sher'ff since way back when, and at his fun'ral, old Mr. Royal took Sher'ff Chamberlin aside and tol' him he wanted him to come back to the county and be sher'ff."

"To run for sheriff, Billy?" inquired Milo. "To leave a secure job and run for sheriff?"

"No, sir, Mr. Moray, sir; you don't unnerstand. See, back then, Mr. Royal, he *owned* this county—lock, stock and barr'l—just like his paw afore him, and his grandpaw and all. Aw, it was elections and all, for the looks of things, but everbody knowed that whosomever Mr. Royal was for, he was gone win whatever he was runnin' for. And all the sher'ff would tell him, they say, was he'd think on it and pray on it and let him know 'bout it.''

Milo chuckled. "That sounds just like the Chamberlin I knew, years back, Billy, damned if it doesn't.''

"Wal,'' continued Crawford, "after a couple of months had gone on and the depities as was running things had fucked up real good and proper a couple times and the fuckin' state police had had to be called into the county one those times and still no word from the sher'ff, old Mr. Royal, he had hisself drove into D.C., had him a confab with some of the big shots the sher'ff worked for, then, then talked to the sher'ff.

"I hear tell the sher'ff wouldn't talk to Mr. Royal alone, naw, had a couple his D.C. officers with him and he laid it on the line to Mr. Royal, too, they say. He told the old man that was he to come out here and be sher'ff, he was gone be sher'ff of all the folks in the county, not just a fuckin' errand boy for the Royal fambly, and that Mr. Royal had best get that straight up front and be ready to sign a witnessed contract that would say that and some other things or he could go back and make one his depities the sher'ff.''

"And what happened then, Billy?" asked Milo.

The slight man grinned, took a sip of beer and shook his scar-shiny head once. "Wal, Mr. Royal, he won't no way use to being talked to that way by hardly nobody and he invited the sher'ff to hell in a fuckin' leaky bucket and stomped out and drove back out here, is what. But then that very next month, the guvamint mens, they caught a passel of moonshiners in the fuckin' act . . . and two of them was county depities. The nextest day after he heard 'bout all that fuckin' shit, Mr. Royal, he went back into

D.C. and ate him a heapin' helpin' of crow. He signed ever'thing he was told to sign and when he come back, the sher'ff come with him.''

Crawford took a real swallow of the beer, refilled his glass from the bottle and went on. ''The sher'ff, he went th'ough his inher'ted hashup like a dose of salts, Mr. Moray, sir. Of the three depities was left, one was prosecuted and sent to jail for stealing from the county and the other two jest lit out for parts unknown. He brung in three retired D.C. cops to help him hold things down, then got Mr. Royal to twist enough tails to get the state police to take on my paw and four other fellers in the next trooper training class they run.

''He made Mr. Royal buy custom police cruisers with lights and sireens and all, got radios put in them and in the office, laid out reg'lar p'trol patterns on a county map and talked Mr. Royal round to paying the depities enough so's they didn't feel 'bliged to steal and take payoffs from roadhouses and cook moonshine jest to make ends meet, no more. Got so, they use to say, ever time the sher'ff he'd call in for another 'pointment for to talk to Mr. Royal, the old man would take to pounding his desk and th'owing things and slamming doors and all and yelling that the sher'ff was out to plumb bankrupt him . . . but he allus saw the sher'ff and talked to him and most allus done whatall the sher'ff wanted, too.

''Mr. Royal's kids had all died before him. His eldest boy was kicked by a hoss and kilt while he was playing polo at some ritzy place in Upper Marlboro, back in the thirties. His next-oldest boy was a bomber pilot that was lost in Europe, somewheres in World War Two, and his youngest boy was kilt in training right at the tag end of that war. His daughter, after she'd got loose from two no-count men she'd married, took to drinking so heavy she'd done had to be locked up in some private sanitarium till she kilt herself one night. Old Miz Royal, she took sick and died 'long 'bout nineteen and fifty, too, so Mr. Royal didn' have no close relatives nowhere, and ever'body just figgered when he come to die, too, it was gonna be some kinda bad shake-up all over the county.

"I tell you, Mr. Moray, sir, it was some damn fuckin' shocked and flat flabbergasted folks here'bouts when his will was read, I tell you, sir. For all he'd spent a lot of time in his last ten or so years yellin' to ever'body could hear him 'bout how the sher'ff was the worstest mistake he'd ever made, was drownedin' him and his corporation and the county in red ink, was mollycoddlin' his damn depities and ridin' roughshod over the better folks in the county, it was none other than Sher'ff Sherwood Chamberlin he left his controllin' int'rest in all three his corporations to."

Milo whistled and shook his head. "So now Chamberlin owns this county, huh?"

"Not really, naw, sir, Mr. Moray," replied Crawford. "He could, and no fuckin' mistake about 'er, was he a mind. But no more'n a week or so after he'd inher'ted ever'thing, he drove down to D.C. and talked to a lot of folks and then talked to folks the first bunch had sent him to and come back up here with a bunch more, one of them a perfessional county manager and the rest either from the state guvamint or the U.S. guvamint. He 'lowed as how it weren't right and proper for no man to die and jest give a whole county and ever'thing in it to another'n, said it won't democratic and that he'd fought a war for democracy and was willing to fight as many more as he had to, come to that. He 'lowed as how nobody should be sher'ff for life, neither, and said the next elections was gonna be honest to God real elections with no fixes on nuthin' or there'd be hell to pay.''

"And yet, I see he's still county sheriff," said Milo, puffing at his old pipe.

"All he's done and seen done for thishere county and all, Mr. Moray, sir," said Crawford, with feeling, "it jest plumb ain't no livin' man anybody'd have for sher'ff but him, Sherwood Chamberlin."

As if on cue, Sherwood Chamberlin opened the door and came back into the private dining room. His face was solemn and his voice, when he spoke, grim. "Milo, Billy, I just got through talkin, to Dr. Kilpatrick, over to County Gen'rul. Bubba Rigny was a DOA—dead on arrival at the emergency room."

Chapter XI

Milo set down his pipe with meticulous care, laid both hands flat on the table and addressed the lawman. "It was self-defense, of course, Chamberlin . . . not that I meant to do more than beat him insensible. I have an attorney in New York City. I'll have to ring him up and get a local recommendation. Whatever the bond is, I can post it; even if I don't have enough cash on me, my attorney can wire me the difference."

"I seen it all, too, Sher'ff, ever' minnit of it," said Crawford, soberly. "Bubba and Wally and Abner set out to beat Mr. Moray and he jest defended hisself, was all. Bubba's beat me a whole hell of a lot worse than Mr. Moray beat him. I'll swear on the Bible to ever' bit of it, too."

Chamberlin picked up his glass of whisky and drained it off with a working of his prominent Adam's apple, then said, "Relax, the both of you, jest relax, hear. If anybody kilt Bubba Rigny, it was Bubba Rigny. Seems he come out of it in the meat wagon, see, and beat up on pore Claude Tatum some kinda bad, then got the damn back door opened and jumped out the meat wagon that was jest then doing over sixty on the fuckin' highway. That alone likely kilt the crazy fucker, but then too one my depities, Chuck Fontaine, was right behind in a cruiser and so close he couldn't help but run right over Bubba's body.''

The lawman shrugged, and as he hooked a finger around the neck of the whisky bottle and began to pour more of the dark-amber fluid into his glass, he declared, ''It's gone hurt Bubba's pore paw and maw and some others, likely, but not as bad prob'ly as it was sure as hell goin' to if he'd lived long enough to do suthin' would see him in the penitent'ry 'stead of jest in my lockup or the county farm, if not the chair or in a state boobyhatch for life. Bubba, he never was strung together too tight, see, Milo; he was a murder jest waitin' to happun from the time he was jest a tad. He got some kinda charge out of hurtin' other folks and animals and all; he was jest born mean, seemed like, and he dint never get no diffrunt or no better. Most his kin wouldn't have ary a particle to do with him from the time he was no more'n ten or twelve; after he beat his pore paw near to death when he was 'bout fourteen, he was put in the reform school for a couple years, but all that seemed to do was make the fucker meaner.

''Whin the war started up and all, lots the young fellers started 'listin', but natcherly, wouldn' any of the services take on Bubba, not with his record. The Marines come closest to takin' him, but fin'ly even they turned him down, and that really tore his asshole, too, 'cause his paw had been a Marine in World War Two and had got shot up on New Georgia Island by the Japs.

''Now, Bubba Rigny'd done beat on Billy, here, afore—hell, big as he allus was for his age, he'd beat on jest 'bout ever'body he'd went to school with—and whin Billy come home on a leave afore he was to be sent over to Vietnam,

Bubba went after him. But this was afore Billy'd done lost part his leg, see, and he'd been taught a whole hell of a lot of hand-to-hand and he ended up putting Bubba in the fuckin' hospital in a fair fight was seed by a dozen or more people. And of course Billy'd done shipped out by the time Bubba was on the street again.

"That Bubba Rigny was jest no good, crazy, no-count; he was headed almost from the day he was borned for a lifer's cell or the 'lectric chair or some pore cop's bullet. This way, the way it went down's for the best, his death cain't be on nobody's conscience, see. It was God's will, is all.''

The copter that lifted off from his uncle's pad beyond the outside swimming pool was not one of the senator's; its three-man crew—despite their carefully tailored clothing and manners as carefully polished as their gleaming shoes— had security bodyguards written all over them in foot-high Day-Glo letters, and James Bedford would have been willing to bet ten years' worth of income that the innocuous-appearing executive copter was not only well armored but was also fitted with a whole plethora of unpleasant and/or fatal surprises for any attacker to encounter.

Soon after he had been seated and served a sealed sipper of hot, fragrant coffee, one of the crew had opened an underseat locker and produced what looked at first to be a small shoulder-strapped lettercase. Going through it slowly, he courteously showed Bedford just how to manipulate the buttons and catches to open it with a slight hiss and disclose a thickly padded interior.

"Now, sir, when you close it back up, be certain to press one or both thumbs on these two buttons. After that, only the imprints of *your* thumbs will be able to release the lock until it is once more opened and reset with another print, you see; anyone who should attempt it will receive a most unhealthy shock.'' The man allowed the ghost of a smile to flit across his face in indication of a species of grim joke.

''You see, sir, as you most likely are aware, the effects of cabin pressurization and depressurization on explosive-tipped small-arms ammunition remains, despite all the advances in weapons technology of late, sometimes distressingly less than pleasant. In the air marshals' cubicle on board the aircraft, you will of course surrender your personal weapons and spare ammo. At that time, you will place the weapons and munitions inside this case and personally secure the catches, then there can be no slightest question that anyone might tinker with your weapons or replace them with other similar ones en route to your destination. Please note down or record the serial number of this case to guard against duplication of cases, for all of this issue are otherwise identical.'' He flitted another smile. ''Government-issue.

''Immediately the cabin has been depressurized, sir, the air marshal will return your cased weapons and you should at that time carefully check them and their loads, actions, et cetera, before reholstering them.

''If, on occasions other than this morning, you are proceeding unescorted through normal airport security, you must report to the air marshal headquarters, display your identification documents and your federal authority to bear weapons, then submit your weapons, ammunition and this case for examination.

''Procedures vary, after all, depending mostly upon the size of the installation. In some of the smaller ones, your weapons will be returned and you will be conducted either to the VIP section or to the plane, if it is ready to board; on board, you will encase your weapons for the on-board marshal as earlier outlined.

"However, in larger installations, you will be expected to encase them in the airport headquarters of the marshals and will then be delivered to the VIP section or plane by way of guarded, armored transport—sometimes ground car or underground rail, sometimes copter.

"Do you have any questions about anything I have described or discussed here this morning, sir? Please feel free to ask me about anything. Being certain that persons such as yourself understand all that must be done is a part of my function."

"Just one, for now," replied Bedford. "What's going to happen when and if I should actually feel constrained to shoot someone? How deep in the soup am I going to be, then?"

The man suffused his voice and manner with infinite reassurance. "Sir, by now every VIP Security headquarters in the country if not the world has been in receipt of a printout of your name, your description, your authorizations and all other pertinent information. Therefore, should you determine termination of someone to be a necessary thing, do so; then you will present the laminated card you were issued to the first person on the scene who produces VIP Security Service identification. Do not surrender your weapon to anyone for any reason unless it is a federal marshal or a properly identified VIPSS representative or operative. Anyone else who demands your weapon without such identification must be considered hostile and so dealt with, up to and certainly including termination by gunfire."

"But what if I make an error of judgment and blow away an innocent party?" probed Bedford. "What happens if I make a snap judgment, say, and shoot one of those murderous little bomblets into a maid or waiter or some tourist asking directions of me?''

The man grimaced, then shrugged. ''Sir, were your particular life and well-being not considered to be of some degree of value to our nation, you would not be in possession of the cards or this case, nor would you be carrying weapons legally or, indeed, flying in this copter and guarded by this team.

''In this twenty-first-century world, humankind are in no way, shape or form considered to be an endangered species and so are not, cannot be considered of comparable importance to someone like you, sir . . . not by anyone with my service or a federal marshal, and only our two services now have any real jurisdiction over you and your defensive actions.''

In other words, Bedford thought with an apprehensive chill, I and anyone else with like credentials am now holder of a license to commit cold-blooded murder. Uncle Taylor is right—this world of ours is become a dangerous jungle and all of us now live under the law of a jungle. How the hell did our United States of America ever come to this?

General Eustace Barstow, U.S.A., or Milo Moray could to some extent have enlightened him in regard to that question, but as the former had died before the turn of the century and the other was out of the country and he never had or was to meet either of them anyway, the question was never resolved in his mind.

Half asleep, Milo received a telepathic beaming from the mother cat in the den area: ''Leader of the two-legs, a mated pair of my kind are in the entry to my den. One of them is of my litter thrown the cold time before the cold time before the cold time before this cold time. They have been told of all you have done for cats, of how you do not seek to kill cats, of your hatred of wolves. They would come close to you and smell you that they better may know you, but you first must open the rock that you used to seal the entry passage.''

Milo was out of the upper bunk in James Bedford's disaster shelter within split seconds and stamping into his boots even as he pulled on his jacket and mentally nudged into wakefulness the other nomads who had occupied the other bunks. Once more thankful for the infiniestimally small periods of time necessary to exchange thoughts and convey messsages in nonspeech mental communication, he explained the situation, reconfirmed his aspirations for both the nomad clans and the cats, then gave his orders that the men should stand ready, awaiting his summons.

Dik Esmith snorted disgustedly aloud while beaming silently, "Ha, Bahb Linsee must be snoring atop the tower rather than keeping watch to not have seen two animals that large not only approach but enter these ruins.''

"Not so," beamed Milo before one of the Linsees could arise in anger to the insult. "Not only must you recall that this night is one of scudding clouds over a moon far from full and bright and that the coats of these cats blends in very well with snow, but also considered that even while injured and hobbling around on three legs, the nursing cat down there managed to steal away a dead deer—a full size, full-grown, adult doe—from under the very noses of us all in broad daylight. Are there no existing circumstances under which you Esmiths and Linsees will cease to pick at and mock and attempt to anger each other like unto so many brattish toddlers? I serve you all fair warning: if your constant, petty, senseless bickerings cost me and the clans the friendship of these cats and their ilk, you will be long in forgetting it and will regret it for the rest of your lives.''

Leaving them all abashed, he strode from the body-heated room out into the chill of the outer chamber, taking one of the gasoline lanterns with him. Within the den area, amid the thick ammonia reek of cat, the cold was bone-deep, but the sinew-cracking effort of raising the ancient steel door on its warped tracks served to suffuse his body with some warmth.

Cued by the recuperating mother cat, he stepped well back from the mouth of the passage and waited. Following a flicker of movement in the dark depths of the low, narrow tunnel, a big, feline head appeared, its three-inch cuspids glinting in the glaring light of the lantern. The yellow-green eyes fixed upon him and he felt the peculiar, familiar tickle in his brain of a new mindspeak.

Lightly, warily, the first cat dropped the two feet from out the tunnel and was followed by a second, this one larger—bigger, bulkier, cuspids thicker and longer by at least a half-inch. Milo had wondered about sexual dimorphism in these strange beasts; now he knew—the male was a third again the size of the female which had led.

''The Mother says that you can communicate with cats, yet you are certainly not a cat, two-legs, so how can this be so?'' asked the newcome feline female, both of them wire-tense, obviously ready to either attack of flee, as they judged best.

''This one cannot say how it is so, cat-sister,'' replied Milo. ''Nonetheless, it is so, as you and your mate can now tell. Nor is this one the only two-legs who can so communicate to those of your kind; within another, smaller den here are other two-legs who have communicated with the Mother and the cubs and can do so with you and your mate, if allowed.''

Slowly, cautiously, the female stalked in a circle around Milo, drawing infinitesimally nearer with each circuit, while the huge male crouched ready to leap upon the two-legs at the first sign of aggression.

Even while stalking, the smaller cat beamed, ''The Mother says that you and the other two-legs have hunted and brought back much meat for her and the new cubs. She says that you slew many, many wolves with your great, long, shiny claw. The Mother says that you and at least one other two-legs did things that took away most of the hurting from her two forepaws. You do not smell very good. You smell more like a wolf than you do like a cat, though not really like a wolf, either. Are you of the breed of two-legs that go about sitting upon the back of fast-running, stupid, hornless four-leg grass-eaters and hurl sharp-pointed sticks at cats and all other ones?''

''The two-legs smells more like a bear than like a wolf,'' put in the male cat. ''Or more like a bear and a boar, together. He does not eat just meat, this cat thinks, yet he is not really a prey-beast, either. What are you, two-legs?''

''Quite true,'' agreed Milo, readily. ''My kind consume both flesh and plants, just as do the bear and the boar, and so it is understandable that our scents would be similar. Yes, my kind do ride upon fast-running four-legs and sometimes hurl sticks with sharp points at beasts of many kinds. We also keep together large numbers of other four-legs grass-eaters—these of some three kinds, all with horns; we keep them for their milk and their meat and for other things useful to us. And we guard them closely from cats, bears and wolves, using to help us guard them four-legs much like wolves but larger and fiercer.

"As to what I am, I and my kind, we are creatures who would be friends and allies of your kind of cats. We would join with you in keeping our mutual bellies filled always, in protecting kittens and cubs of both our kinds. I will freely admit that I do not know if it would work out, if it can be done; but such an alliance would benefit both two-legs and cats in many, many ways, and I would be more than willing to try to make such an arrangement work."

"Perhaps we should just kill him and see if he tastes as foul as he smells?" the female half-questioned the waiting male.

From out the darkness of the den area, the nursing cat came hobbling on her still-healing legs. "Then you must kill this cat, too," she snarled. "This two-legs has cared for me and my cubs, has hunted for us all and has protected us from the wolves when this cat was too hurt to do so herself. Were he a cat, he now would be my mate, but mate or not, cat or not, I will stand by him in any fight."

And also from out the darkness of the den-area came stalking, stiff-legged and as threatening as a bristling, snarling, thirty pounds of cub could make himself appear, Killer-of-Two-Legs beaming, "And you must kill this cat, also . . . if you can."

James Bedford had been aware that his original hotel reservations had been canceled and that new reservations for him had been booked at a security hotel in the greater Miami area, but it had not been until he actually arrived that he had become aware that the particular security hotel was the Jupiter Offshore Resort Hotel—unreachable save by air, expected surface vessel or the undersea-rail system.

As another VIPSS copter dropped down toward the landing pads atop the spreading hostelry, Bedford regarded the overt armaments placed here and there ready to repel hostile visitors—whether airborne or seaborne—and wondered just how much good any of them would do in event of a hurricane, not even to mention such other natural disturbances as tsunamis, tornados or earth tremors. At that moment, he really yearned for the safe, almost uninhabited isolation of the far-western mountains, where he could go about unarmed without fear or bodyguards.

To the young man beside him—virtually a clone of the one who had flown with him from his uncle's home to the D.C. airport somewhat earlier in the day—he said, "I wish I could've been put up on the mainland, closer to the main business area. These offshore things give me the willies, especially down here in the heart of the hurricane belt. How many were lost back in 'oh-one, when the Kitty Hawk Offshore went under?"

The man shrugged and flitted a brief smile of the kind that seemed to be a mark of his profession—boyish, charming, very reassuring. "You should not worry yourself, sir. Remember, the regrettable disaster of which you speak—the Kitty Hawk thing—that complex was one of the first of its kind built, and it had not, it was subsequently discovered, been properly maintained, not been renovated to keep it abreast of modern technological advances, as it should have been . . . as it would have been, had my service been connected with it.

"The Jupiter, here, now, is something else, and I speak of personal experience when I say so, sir. I happened to be here on bodyguard duty during the bad hurricane of 'oh-six. Yes, there was some exterior damage to the structure—the surface-docking facilities were torn away or sunk, the subsurface system was damaged and rendered temporarily inoperable from either end, a few of the air-defense pods were damaged or blown off—but inside the entire complex there might have been nothing more life-threatening than a half-gale blowing around the outer surfaces; indeed, there were parties being held in almost all the guest areas during the very worst of the storm.''

Again, the trace of a reassuring smile. ''Besides, there is presently not even a tropical depression listed, much less any storm activity or threat, sir. And these offshore complexes have proved far easier to render secure than even the best-planned or -built mainland units. Here at Jupiter we have what amounts to a security complex within a basically secure complex. There is no way in which anyone or anything can come into or go out of this main complex without being closely observed and monitored . . . ever, under any circumstances.

''The complex is virtually self-sufficient. A small, well-shielded nuclear pile provides all power for whatever purposes, there are vast stocks of food and supplies, fresh water comes either from distillation of salt water or from an artesian well tapping Pleistocene water a thousand feet below the continental shelf, though it is not generally used because of the terrible shortage of fresh, potable water in Florida, overcrowded as the state is, these days.

''There are no less than six heated saltwater pools within this complex, two of them within the security subcomplex. Also, two of the restaurants are wholly within our confines, along with numerous other facilities. Moreover, because of the singular nature of this type of operation, we can confidently assure real and complete security to all our

VIP guests, and that is something that neither we nor any other service can or could offer in even the most carefully guarded mainland facility anywhere in the nation, if not the world, sir.

"So safe are you here at Jupiter, sir, that you do not even need any personal weapons . . . although you will not be requested to surrender them, of course."

Bedford did not get to see any of the main resort complex that day; he was conveyed directly from the helipad into the reception area of the security module, properly identified, and then courteously conducted to what they called an executive mini-suite. The suite was far from large, as compared with such accommodations on the mainland, but it included the utterly last words in luxurious appointments, and Bedford only hoped that as his uncle had booked it, he was paying for it, too, for as the finances of the group now stood, he and they could not afford such opulence.

"Again, thank you, Dr. Harrel/Markov," he hissed to himself, aloud and with intense venom. "You and your damned spendthrift nature and your triple-damned Project *latifrons* has very nearly ended the group before it fairly began to do anything worthwhile."

A soft tone and a blink of subdued light emanated just then from the communications console and a female voice as soothing as warm honey intoned, "Mr. Bedford, you have a call from a Senator Bedford, in Washington, D.C., on the videophone. If you wish scrambling, you will have to do without the video aspect of the call."

"Did the caller request scrambling?" asked Bedford.

"No, sir," replied the disembodied voice.

"Then I can do without it, thank you," said Bedford. "You may put it through to me, please."

Taylor Bedford appeared on the screen, smiling. "You arrived safely, then, James. Good."

"Yes," agreed James, "but I may be washing dishes for the next ten years or more before they let me leave here, the Jupiter Complex. This place looks far too rich for my group to afford for even a few days."

Taylor Bedford chuckled. "Don't worry about it, James. You are in the suite I usually use down there, and the costs will all go on my account . . . call it a part of my loan to you.

"But such matters aside. I now have some answers for you as to the incident that precipitated your current need for security and secure accommodations. Pick up the receiver of the dark-green audio set—I am going to play a tape for you and I do not think it should air unscrambled. After you've heard it, I'll speak with you again."

As the screen went blank, James Bedford lifted the indicated receiver and placed it to his ear to hear a very deep voice begin to speak in Russian. "Mr. Bedford, because your most distinguished uncle, the Senator Taylor Bedford, has told me that you understand my beautiful language, I will not need to assault you with my less than perfect English.

"Mr. Bedford, my name is Piotr Barislev and I am speaking to you from my office in the embassy of the Union of the Soviet Socialist Republics, here in Washington, District of Columbia. I sincerely wish that I could assure you that no Russian had any part in the disgraceful attempt to kidnap you and possibly harm you which took place in this city so short a time ago, but unfortunately, such is not the case.

"Nonetheless, please be certainly assured that only a small, counterproductive and basically criminal element was involved. Even as I here speak to you, our internal security forces are rooting out everyone connected with this anti-international, hooligan scheme, both here and in our Motherland. Please believe me when I say that they all, when once apprehended, will be tried and severely punished for their transgressions and attempted transgressions.

"Despite the true fact that they did not in any way represent anything approaching official policy, they were still Russian nationals and, therefore, our responsibility while they were upon the soil of your beautiful country, and so I hereby offer to you, Mr. Bedford, the full, sincere and most abject apology of the ambassador, the vice-ambassadors, myself and all other officials and staff of our embassy. Whenever we can do anything of any sort to even partially recompense you for your mistreatment, please do not hesitate to so inform me. Your distinguished uncle will know how to contact me or you may ask for me, here at the embassy, if you wish.

"Before I ring off, if you know the present whereabouts of a Russian scientist who may be claiming Israeli citizenship, one Dr. Vasili Markov or possibly Harel, please inform us or your so distinguished uncle. We are most anxious to find this man and to remove him back to Russia to stand trial with his fellow criminals and share in their punishments."

There followed a bit of mechanical noise, then Taylor Bedford's well-modulated voice said, "Before you ask, yes, you can believe Comrade Barislev . . . well, as much as you can believe any of them, of his stripe, that is. The way I hear it, the whole security network over there at that embassy complex are mad as hops and getting madder as they squeeze more info out of the ones they've caught to date. They have a security apparatus firmly fixed in place, and they don't need and certainly want a pack of Russian amateurs playing their own undercover games out of the same embassy, which is what it would appear this whole stinking mess was . . . here again, if you can believe everything they say about it.

"Thus far, in addition to the botched try for you, Barislev avers that this bunch have been responsible for two attempted kidnappings of some Canadian scientist—once in Canada, once in this country—a possible murder in Greece, an attempted murder in Israel, and some thefts of replication-related material here and there around the world, and they speculate that the same bunch or their agents may have been the ones who snatched the South African in Switzerland, collected a quite sizable ransom, then dumped his dead body into Lake Geneva. Not only that—and I didn't get this from Barislev—it would seem that the core group of this lot had arranged to sell or assign some replication rights for themselves, bypassing the Russian government, which is a definite no-no."

"And Harel is involved in this?" asked James Bedford.

"It would seem so," the senator replied. "Rather deeply involved, I would imagine, based on Barislev's real eagerness to catch up to the man."

"Then God help him," said James, with feeling. "I detest him, but . . ."

"God is about the only force that could help him," remarked his uncle dryly, "with the KGB sniffing on his heels. They're most efficient, you know, James, and, not to accuse them of ruthlessness, they play rough, to win, no matter what the cost."

"Then the danger to me is over, I take it?" inquired James Bedford. "I can stop carrying this bomb-loaded pistol and move over to a normal hotel on the mainland and stop tripping over security types every time I turn around, Uncle Taylor?''

''Uhh, not quite yet, James,'' came the reply. ''For one thing, Barislev and the Russians still don't know for sure just how many people were involved in this thing of theirs. Moreover, our own types have come up with another foreign group that has evinced more than just a passing interest in you and your movements, of late. I don't know exactly who this group is or represents—the VIPSS won't tell even me, which could mean a lot or nothing at all—but they seem to be some worried, and anything that worries them should certainly worry me . . . and you, especially. So keep your pistol loaded and on you, at least within reach, at all times, keep your eyes open and don't try to slip away from those who are there to protect you. Be a good boy and maybe you'll live to see that cat species replicated yet . . . if the world we know doesn't end first, that is.

''Good night, now, James. Have a few drinks and a good dinner and get some sleep. I'll be in touch.''

Bedford hung up and sat back to try to think out all that he had heard from his uncle and the deep-voiced Russian, but before he could even begin to order his thoughts, the same soft tone and light presaged the warm-honey voice which announced, ''Mr. Bedford, the early seating will commence in the White Fleet Club in three-quarters of an hour. A printout of the evening menu may be obtained by means of following the instructions to be found in the VIP Guest Packet. However, please allow us to strongly recommend the Severn Terrapin. If you wish to dine in your suite, you may place your order in one-quarter hour and expect service within an hour. The Carronade Lounge is currently open, both the bar and the appetizer buffet.''

Never having developed a taste for raw fish, Bedford passed by the section of the buffet devoted to sashimi and finally served himself grilled crayfish tails in a torrid sauce, a few bite-size nuggets of curried alligator and a few crackers to go with his brandy and soda.

He had downed the most of the nibbles and about half the drink and was interestedly eyeing an attractive woman of about his own age who sat listening to a vaguely familiar older man and now and then nodding her head of dark curls when he felt rather than saw a presence nearby.

''Mr. James Bedford?'' asked the tall, blond, elegant-seeming man. ''You are Mr. James Bedford, who represents the Stekowski group?''

Hurriedly chewing and swallowing, Bedford nodded once. ''Yes, I'm Bedford, Mr . . . ?''

With a click of the heels and a short, perfunctory bow, the man said, ''I am *Doktor* Erich von Kurfuerst. We share mutual interests. Would you join me for dinner this evening, please?''

Chapter XII

Slowly, ever so slowly, with many a stop and start, the winter was relaxing its cruel, deadly grip on the plateau and the surrounding montane wilderness. Though meltwaters that rushed and pooled deeply during the days always still froze over at night, some of the days were sunny-warm in comparison to the long cold that gradually was dissipating.

It was none too soon for Milo and his nomads, either, for—despite the necessary hunts they had undertaken in order to keep both themselves and the cats fed adequately—the long confinement inside the ruins was resulting in severe cabin fever and resultant ill-humor and short tempers.

More important to Milo, who intended to get as much as possible of the many-volume Bedford Journal read before the clans arrived, the supply of gasoline for the lanterns was running perilously low; therefore, immediately he thought it possible, he rigged a movable windbreak on the top of the brick tower and thenceforth spent much of many sunny days reading by natural light, often joined by one or more of the growing cubs and, less frequently, by their mother or one or both of the newcome adult cats. The cats usually did little more than curl up and snooze; nonetheless, the still-biting gusts of air that sometimes found a way around the windbreak frequently made him glad for the nearby sources of body heat.

Because the recuperating mother cat's forelegs still were not equal to absorbing the necessary shock of her not inconsiderable weight after a drop of the more than eight feet from the tower top to the platform below it, he used a mostly cloudy day to take all the nomads, a coil of strong rope and a couple of the fine, sharp twenty-first-century axes down into the woods just below the plateau. There they felled and roughly trimmed a sizable pine tree, then managed to get it up one side of the sheer wall of rock and snaked it across the soggy ground to lean it against the tower and so provide easy access and egress to or from the tower top for any beast with claws.

While they were at the welcome exertion, they dismantled the yurt left below by the clansmen visitors (left behind in order to pack more wolf skins on the packhorses), then hoisted it, too, up onto the plateau. That night, even Milo willingly forewent the bunk beds in the disaster shelter in order to huddle on the cold ground inside the familiar, homey, unconfining confines of the simple felt yurt.

As the deep layers of ice and snow began to melt away from first the tower and then an ever widening periphery of the ruins, Milo and the nomads went about finding thawing, hideless wolf carcasses and dragging them to where they could be cast over the verges of the plateau before they thawed out, decomposed and not only made the environs of the ruins unbearable with the stench but attracted all manner of scavengers and noxious insects to the feast.

From the very first attempt, the men had all discovered that the two adult cats were, with their telepathy, an invaluable pair of hunting partners. Hunting in company with one of them made the hunting much easier on both men and cat and far more certain of edible conclusions. The men, armed with bows and spears, needed only to spot the prey beasts, position themselves and then have the cat or cats circle around so as to show themselves or give the game their scent or mock-charge them into fleeing in panic past the positions taken by the waiting men. It was relaxed, almost completely dangerless hunting, and all parties seemed to enjoy it.

After the first experience, however, neither of the big cats would accompany any hunting party that included Milo, not when he chanced to arm himself with the ancient rifle and his dwindling stock of cartridges; the flat crack of shots hurt their ears, they beamed bluntly, going on to beam that if the two-legs wanted to accompany another two-legs carrying such an insufferably loud, smelly thing, they were welcome to do so, but that no sensible cat could or should be expected to willingly subject itself to such sensory abuse.

With a shrug, Milo cleaned and oiled the fine weapon, then repacked it and the thirteen remaining cartridges for it back in the way he had found them. The cats were worth far more to him and the clans, now, than the use of an archaic hunting rifle. Without a doubt, the rifle's barrel could have been worked into a fine blade for sword or saber by a Horseclans smith and the smaller metal parts into many other useful item, tool or weapon, but the rifle had served him and the nomads and the cats well, had saved their lives from the huge, ravenous pack of wolves that had cornered them up there in these ruins and was sitting siege on them all, and he was sufficiently sentimental to return it to where he had so fortuitously discovered it in their time of dire need, to let it go back to its ages-long rest to await there the improbable finding of it by another who might know what it was and how to use it and be in need of its awesome, deadly power.

Questioning of the cats relative to the existences and the possible locations of others of their kind was tricky and not very rewarding, Milo had discovered. The big adult male recalled first awareness in surroundings that, from his hazy description, Milo could only assume had been a cave in some mountainside, but what side of what mountain and where from here that mountain might lie were questions that the massive beast could neither answer nor really grasp as important. Apparently, he had left his parents and siblings—his pride?—when he became sexually mature and so presented an incipient threat to his sire. He had hunted alone for either two or three cold times before finding scent of his present mate. Their last year's litter had all died of mishap before becoming more than mere cubs, and so poor had been the hunting this terrible winter—before they had wandered into this area and found no recent signs of a territorial resident—that she had not gone into estrus.

The female, for her part, had seen no cats of her sort other than her mate since wandering off from the ruin two cold-times in the past, but she did recall having smelled the relatively recent presence of two others of her kind in her circuits, though—most frustrating for Milo—she recalled neither where nor when and finally stalked off when he kept probing at the matter. Feline priorities, he reflected, differed markedly from those of his kind.

"The only answer, I guess," Milo thought, "is to keep the clans in this general vicinity for as long as I can, this year, winter on those cold plains down there again, then come back up here and keep doing that until we can gather a decent-sized breeding stock of these intelligent, tele-pathic cats . . . either that or take the chance of trying to make it with what we have on hand, all but one of which are very closely related. Hell, all of them may be for all I or anyone else knows of it, really knows of it.

"Interesting and really fascinating as are Bedford's var-ied experiences away back when, much as I enjoy reading them through, I do wish he'd get into a little more detail about the replication of this *Panthera feethami* a little more quickly, for perhaps if I knew a bit more about the particu-lar types of cats that were used in that replication experi-ment, I'd be better able to judge how and where to find these existing cats. Are these the descendants of those? Hell, what else could they be, pray tell? At one time or another, back then, in the twentieth and twenty-first centu-ries, I was in various parts of five continents and I never saw or heard of the like of these cats, not living ones. And even as sparsely settled as this area was back then, it was pretty thoroughly hunted each year, and no large predator such as these cats with their thick, beautiful, stunning coats and those distinctive fangs would've been unnoticed and at least reported by a hunter or ranger.

"He's already noted his buying of two replicated cave lions, and these present cats seem to live at least in family groups, as lions do, too; furthermore, the adult male's family did live in a cave, rather than just use it for bearing and weaning of a litter, such as other cats and, for that matter, not a few other animals of many kinds do. I just know too little right now to know how much I need to know, yet, I guess. So I suppose it must be back to the Bedford Journal, for me.

"But there're other problems, too. This trouble that the clans have experienced this winter with indigeneous nomads means that if we're going to stay up in this neck of the woods for the length of time we may need to if we're going to go about rooting out cats, we're going to be obliged either to hammer out a way to peacefully coexist with the locals or actively make full-scale war on them to the point where we wipe them out or drive them elsewhere. Of the two latter alternatives, the first is preferable, I've found in similar cases over the years; driven out, they can always lick at their wounds, regroup and come back at you, come back mad for your blood; wiped out, they'll be done for—well-hacked, arrow-quilled corpses never regroup and counterattack anyone.

"Naturally, I'd much liefer make peace with them, at least. Or better, join them with my people, my Horseclans, just as I did with the Scotts and the Lindsays and not a few before them; there're still not all that many human beings left on earth that we can afford to butcher large numbers on anything approaching the scale of warfare during the last century of the old world, the old civilization's horrendous wars. But much as I'd like it, as much real sense as it makes under the circumstances and in light of mankind's drastically reduced numbers on the face of the land, it still may not be possible, may not work in this case, with this particular group or groups of people; old General Eustace Barstow hit the nail squarely on the head when he averred that mankind was grossly misnamed, that, indeed, he was the least kind and the most savage, cruel and unremittingly bloodthirsty of all the creatures on the planet, more bestial than any beast, never forgetting, never forgiving, ever able to recall or imagine a good excuse for slaughter of his own kind or any other, seldom allowing either age or sex to stand in the way of his insatiable bloodlust.

"Well, his world, the one he tried so hard and so vainly to save, ended just about as he predicted it would end, and that end only missed his timetable by a few, a very few, years, too. It's such a goddam pity that more people couldn't have seen, have realized just how right that man and the handful of ones of like mind were in time to have joined with them and saved that world, maybe have kept it and its technology and its institutions going long enough to find a way to cure humanity of its savagery.

"Reading Bedford's reminiscences, through these long weeks, I'm recalling so much, so very much, of my own life, my own experiences in the dear, dead world. There was a lot of good in it, despite all the undeniable cruelties and horror and inhumanity. Even within the less than a century of it that I recall, things had gotten better in many, many ways for a wide swath of human beings around that world.

"Yes, millions starved to death, but those that did so did so either because they bred unchecked until there were too many of them for the land to support, because they were on marginal land to begin or because of the mismanagement—sometimes the deliberate and cruelly calculated mismanagement—of governmental structures or regimes. In any case, the overall percentage of people who starved to death in that world in those times was far and away lower than those who died similarly in earlier, less technological times on the planet.

"So terribly much would've, could've been different and better if there had been one overpoweringly strong and, more important, resolute and determined government to take control of the world in the wake of World War

Two, point it in the proper path and ride tight herd on all of it until it was firmly set in its course. It was what Eustace Barstow wanted the United States of America to do, what it should've done, even if that had then meant pasting the holy living hell out of Josef Stalin and 'our brave Russian ally.' Though that might not've been necessary, at that point in time, for we had the Bomb then and they didn't; moreover, for all its size, if we'd stopped supplying the Russian Red Army, it would quickly have ground to a halt long before it could've raped its way across Poland and eastern Germany.

"Father Karl, that slimy little pervert, the one we called Padre in the Munich operation at the end of that war, was horrified in my first conversation with him that Barstow might persuade the Powers-that-then-were to do just that, to use our then awesome military force to establish hegemony over the world and all its people. Of course, the reason he was so horrified is that he was plugging something similar—a bastard mixture of Moscow and the Papacy to take over and run the world. That was years before he gave up on the Papacy entirely, in favor of the Kremlin's variety of Communism. Oh, how I wish I'd strangled the skinny swine in Munich, or given one of the DPs a pack of cigarettes to do it for me—how much misery I would've saved myself and who knows how many others, over the years.

"But he's gone now—good riddance to filthy sewage, in his particular case—and so are Barstow and Bedford and all the other people who were of that world, except for me . . . and, maybe, Clarence Bookerman and, to believe what he wrote, possibly one or two more like us, somewhere.

"And if Barstow and his few had succeeded, where would I be now? What would I be doing? If he had really succeeded, had gotten the world into the shape it would've had to be maintained in to survive, there would be no need of small private armies, no small insurrections to be put down here and there every few years in out-of-the-way, generally unpleasant parts of the globe, so surely I wouldn't be plying the trade I followed for most of the time after the U.S. Army decided I was too old to longer serve.

"Well, whatever and wherever, I wouldn't've been hurting for living expenses, good old Jethro Stiles saw to that much, long, long ago. No, I'd most likely have not been soldiering, training soldiers or teaching others how to properly train them, going from continent to continent, nation to nation, war to insurrection to guerrilla as I did for so long; but even so I might well have had to follow the course that Bookerman did: living in areas until too many people were become aware that I didn't age, then moving on, changing my name and identity, only to have to move on again after a few years or a couple of decades, at the very most, tops.

"Over the years, since he decamped so precipitously, back in Kansas . . . or was it Nebraska? I can't now recall . . . I've often wondered about him, speculated on the forces that shaped him, that so warped him as to make him a still-fervent adherent of German National Socialism while seemingly completely forgetting, mentally blanking out, all of the horrors attendant to that ill-conceived, ill-starred philosophy and regime, even scores of years after its overdue demise.

"I've just about come to the conclusion that it was the constant moving, the rootlessness, the never-ending fear of apprehension by civil or, worse, ecclesiastical authorities, the endless round of losing all whom he held dear, respected or loved that brought him to cling so passionately to Adolf Hitler and his cause, immediately he discovered Hitler to be such a one as himself . .. and, God help me, like me, too, if he guessed right.

"Hitler, the National Socialist German Workers' Party, and the Third German Reich became in Bookerman's mind, then, not simply a cause but truly a family—the loved and cherished family he had for so long sought and been denied. People, even my kind of people, tend to magnify the good and gloss over the bad qualities of those they love and cherish, and so did Bookerman with his 'family.' In his eyes, his mind, Hitler could not possibly do anything wrong, all of his aims were lofty, exalted.

"Clarence Bookerman is not, himself, a bad or an evil man, I believe, I have come to believe. He is brilliant, multitalented, a worthy product of the Renaissance that spawned him; he is, can be, generous, compassionate, self-sacrificing and intensely loyal to those he feels deserving or needful, and all of these have always been considered to be commendable qualities for any human being to possess. Yes, admitted, he can be narrow and very cruel, too, but in all the cases I saw of him, only in regard to his loyalties, to those he knew to be dependent upon him and his protection.

"An excellent case in point is what he did to that bushwhacker we captured in Colorado. God, it was gutwrenching to have to watch and hear while he used a stainless-steel teaspoon to take out that bastard's eyeball—especially so for me, since I knew just how it felt to have eyes gouged out, the damned Vietminh having done that and other things to me before they shot me and left me for dead after I'd escaped from Dien Bien Phu.

"What Bookerman did on that day so tore up and alienated Gus Olsen and Harry Krueger that neither of them ever after that would have any more to do with Clarence than absolutely necessary. But what he did was the only thing that would have worked to break that tough young bastard, that got for us the location of the place in which his gang of marauders had holed up and enabled us to surprise them and slaughter them, removing a deadly menace that could well have cost the lives of most or all of our people, had it been allowed to continue to exist.

"And then there were so many other things he did for the good of our people, such as boiling old, hellishly unstable dynamite in order to render out and provide us with nitroglycerin with which to attack the camp of that same bunch of bushwhackers in Colorado, or insisting to be the one to be put out on the prairie alone and beyond any sort of assistance in order to test out that first felt yurt he'd designed and put together, and so planned it as to ride out a terrible blizzard out there in isolation. Those are examples of selflessness and very real concern if such ever existed, to my way of thinking.

"But Gus and Harry never could seem to understand, after that one terrible incident, and I think that in large measure, their unceasing animosity and uncompromising distrust of him and anything that he suggested or did was a primary reason that he left us when and as he did. I, at least, know and recognize and acknowledge the patent debt we all owe Dr. Clarence Bookerman, for without his experiments and the notes he left for me to find, the survival of the group whose descendants are become the Horseclans would've been a very chancy, iffy thing, indeed.

"Nomadic life is hard—always has been, always will be—the mortality rate is high, the suffering severe, so that even with a bit of an edge on survival, only the very toughest ever live long enough to breed more of their rugged kind. Aspects of Bookerman's unquestioned genius, it was, that gave the Horseclans progenitors that precious edge.

"They might've still survived, some of them anyway, with only my guidance, true. But despite my years of warring and hunting all over the world, I still was basically a creature of the then-recent past—of the late twentieth and very early twenty-first centuries—and, as such, far too dependent upon manufactured chemicals, drugs and equipment to have done those people all that much good in their initial, desperate struggles to adapt, to learn to survive their new, incredibly rugged life as herders on the prairie, lacking almost everything they needed in the beginning, especially the knowledges of how to adapt naturally occurring items to their needs.

"Bookerman, on the other hand, could draw upon the personal and empiric knowledge of centuries rather than just some few mere scores of years.

"From the few hints I heard from him and read in his letter and notes, I think he must have lived through at least a part of the seventeenth century and, certainly, through all of the eighteenth, nineteenth and twentieth, so he had memories of how things had been done, made, fashioned and from what raw materials before the industrial age, even, much less the technological age. It was these memories, plus his spate of experiments, that made his notebooks so precious to the people he left in my care.

"I wonder if *he* has survived? Probably. I wonder just where he is now. What he's doing? I wonder if ever I'll run across him again, too, I wonder that often. I sure hope so.

"Back to the cats, now. They, too, could be a very definite survival edge for the Horseclans. People used to state that as opposed to dogs, horses and other domestic animals, cats were untrainable, sneaky and unreliable if not inherently vicious, and they were right . . . as far as they took their argument and the thoughts behind it.

"Cats are indeed different from dogs or any others of the so-called domestic animals; I recall reading once that the cat tribe constitute the epitome of predator development, are one of the most highly evolved forms of mammal, very adaptable and so able to live and breed in a vast range of habitats—subarctic to tropic, swamp to desert, mountain to prairie. From a cave in a ruin to a yurt on the plains? Maybe.

"Unlike a dog, which will learn to do just about anything to please its master, will quickly adapt its life-style to fit that same master's, cats own their own, peculiar set of priorities and will seldom forgo any of those feline imperatives for any other creature or purpose.

"Your cat has a principal imperative of keeping its belly full of high-protein food, and it knows it must feed and care for its young, protect them until they are big enough to see to their own needs. Cats sleep or rest a great deal and possess relatively little stamina over a long haul, so they must have a safe, secure or guarded place to sleep and must obtain their necessary high-protein food with as little stress and danger as possible. They feel pain and suffering as keenly as any animal and they naturally try to avoid anything that would hurt or injure them.

"These two, this mated pair of this singular kind of long-fanged cat, have adapted to hunting in concert with me and the other men simply because I was able to convince them, to show them, that it was to their advantage to do so as much as it was to ours. This way, they get their bellies filled on a fairly regular basis with the kinds of food best suited to them and they do so with far less exertion and danger of injury than they would've had they been doing the usual kind of feline hunting—the kind of tooth-and-claw killing that cost the life of the Mother's mate and her own crippling injury. The stalk always takes a long while, and it therefore burns up energy, but the most dangerous moments of a hunt—dangerous to the cat or cats—is always the kill, when it is of necessity close enough to be itself killed or crippled by the horns, hooves, teeth or sheer strength of its prey. Hunting in cooperation with us has not only shortened the stalking time, it has eliminated physical risk to the cats, and for these reasons they are more than willing to continue with us as hunting companions.

"They also seem to have quickly learned that it is safe to sleep nearby us, that we not only will not ourselves harm them, but that we will protect them from any other living creature, so they have come to feel safe and secure with us here.

"My next task, of course, is going to be to try to sell them and their certain value to the rest of the clansfolk . . . and the rest of the clansfolk to them. It will help that so many Horseclansfolk own at least some degree of telepathy and so, conceivably, will be able to actually communicate, mind to mind, with these cats, as they can none of them—or me, either, for that matter—with our dogs and hounds. If these strange cats are as intelligent as I think they are, that will help, too."

He chuckled to himself, thinking, "The next clan to join us may be a clan composed of sizable, four-legged, furry clansfolk with fur and claws and fangs—the Clan of the Cats."

ABOUT THE AUTHOR

ROBERT ADAMS lives in Seminole County, Florida. Like the characters in his books, he is partial to fencing and fancy swordplay, hunting and riding, good food and drink. At one time Robert could be found slaving over a hot forge, making a new sword or busily reconstructing a historically accurate military costume, but, unfortunately, he no longer has time for this as he's far too busy writing.

HORSECLANS FANS PLEASE NOTE:

For more information about Milo Morai, Horseclans, and forthcoming Robert Adams books contact the NATIONAL HORSECLANS SOCIETY, P.O. Box 1770, Apopka, FL 32704-1770.